Praise for Amy Mistretta's *Undying Passions*

"UNDYING PASSIONS is a spine chilling mystery filled with terror and emotions that jumps off of its pages. ...a riveting novel full of suspects and hidden secrets that at times both shock and surprise its reader with their intensity. Coupled with an erotic punch that cannot be denied as these two lost loves reconnect. ...Danger, sex and a love that never died combine to make UNDYING PASSIONS a keeper that should be enjoyed again and again."

   ~ Jenn L., Romance Junkies

"Undying Passions is a very passionate story... The suspenseful tension is quite pronounced. The intriguing plot is interesting, moving at a steady pace with no slow parts or lags in the action. The story is well written and the timing of the unfolding mysteries from the past and present are perfectly executed. Undying Passions is a great read that I highly recommend."

   ~ Karen H., The Romance Studio

Look for these titles by
Amy Mistretta

Now Available:

Secrets Within
Alone in Forrester Rock

Undying Passions

Amy Mistretta

A Samhain Publishing, Ltd. publication.

Samhain Publishing, Ltd.
577 Mulberry Street, Suite 1520
Macon, GA 31201
www.samhainpublishing.com

Undying Passions
Copyright © 2008 by Amy Mistretta
Print ISBN: 978-1-59998-824-5
Digital ISBN: 1-59998-567-5

Editing by Imogen Howson
Cover by Scott Carpenter

First Samhain Publishing, Ltd. electronic publication: September 2007
First Samhain Publishing, Ltd. print publication: July 2008

Dedication

To those who have loved and lost... Whether it's rekindled through an old flame or ignited by a new passion, love will find you again.

Chapter One

Tess Fenmore slouched behind the steering wheel of her car, staring out the windshield, the funeral home across the street taunting her with regret. All the pent-up anguish had nothing to do with the building but rather with the man inside.

Johnny Sawyer.

At one time, Tess had loved him so much and for years, memories of Johnny had driven her crazy. She hadn't been able to get him out of her mind.

Even though he had made one hell of a mess out of her life.

Through months of heavy tears, she had tried moving on, but to this day the pain was still there. Deeply. It only proved she had never gotten over him.

Feeling the pain of her past as the sun beat down through the windshield, still staring at the gloomy funeral home, Tess wiped back a stray tear. The old memories didn't seem old any more.

She wished she could banish them from her mind altogether, do away with every person in her life who had wronged her. Every time she found herself reminiscing, Tess felt the twinge in her gut from what she had walked in on that day long ago.

She placed her head on the steering wheel, closing her eyes, willing the images from her past to go away.

But they never did.

The hardest thing was, year after year, Johnny and Tess had continued living in the same town. It always struck her as funny to see how two people who were once close could live far apart with nothing more than a stolen glance shared between them. Yet the ache remained, seeing him move on with his life.

One more person who had thrown her away.

The hurt was as fresh as if it happened yesterday. However, it happened eleven years ago, and Tess couldn't understand why the feeling of betrayal still lingered deep within her heart, persisting to haunt her.

It took all the emotional strength Tess had to put the car in gear and drive to the parking lot across the street. Feeling as though she were bordering on the edge of a cliff, her emotions threatening to come crashing around her, tears stinging her eyes, blurring her vision, she parked the car.

When Tess walked into the funeral home, feeling uncomfortable, alone, as though she had no right being there, people stared, their whispers unmistakable, probably wondering why after all these years she would show up at the wake.

Despite their intentness, Tess pushed forward. She had to do this, had to face the past, pay her final respects, more so for herself than for any other reason.

Suddenly, she stopped, her feet frozen to the dark-colored carpet beneath her. There he was. The time that had passed between them had been so long. To see him like this...

It was devastating.

No matter what was going on inside her head, Tess had to

be strong, had to go to him, to Johnny Sawyer, who stood alone next to his wife's coffin.

Tess approached the casket.

Other than a slight sideward glance, she tried keeping her gaze off Johnny as he stared, startled by her sudden presence. Kneeling down on the small wooden step, Tess said a prayer. Not a prayer filled with her forgiveness, just the simplest goodbye to someone who had once been an important part of her life.

Lindsey Moran...Tess's one-time best friend, now Lindsey Sawyer, a woman who had deceived her in the worst possible way.

If it hadn't been for the destructive thunderstorm, or the sharpness of the bend in the road, Tess wouldn't have had a reason to be there.

She'd heard about the tragedy on the local radio station the morning after. A car had been traveling at high speed along a country road, when it veered off the shoulder. Why had Lindsey been driving so fast? Was her car the only one involved? The police would never know.

It was irrelevant now.

Lindsey Sawyer had been pronounced dead at the scene of the accident, the impact of the crash too much for her body to handle and the internal bleeding irreversible. The broadcast reported that the rescue team had been forced to call in the Jaws of Life to get her out of the mangled car.

The only thing that brought Tess out of shock that morning, after hearing Lindsey's name come through the speakers of her radio, had been the sound of her coffee mug shattering on the kitchen floor.

Although it was true that Tess had never forgiven Lindsey for crossing the line, destroying their friendship forever, she

11

wouldn't wish such pain or eternal heartache on anyone.

Not even Johnny Sawyer.

Her mind was free of all thoughts of betrayal, rather filled with warm memories of Lindsey. From the times they had played together on the school playground, their prom, graduation... But no matter how hard she tried, the pain came back in full with the vision of seeing Lindsey in bed with Johnny.

Even in death, the thoughts, the images, couldn't be banished.

After privately saying her peace, Tess started to turn, to head back down the aisle and out the door. Except she couldn't. She faced Johnny with sadness in her eyes, a kind of sadness she couldn't explain.

Tess walked to him, reached out and took his hand.

His body was shaking, shaking badly. He didn't turn away. At that moment, Tess wanted nothing more than to take him in her arms, to hold him, to comfort Johnny in any way she could.

The feeling had nothing to do with her past love for him, but rather a need to ease his pain. Unfortunately, it wasn't that simple. No matter what she said—or did—nothing would change the fact that he would have to bury his wife the next day.

"Thanks for coming, Tess. It means a lot."

"I'm so sorry."

She had always thought that particular phrase at a funeral was repetitious, but now she knew why people said it. What more could you possibly say to someone who'd had their whole world taken from them?

"She would've been happy to know that you came." Johnny looked from Tess down to Lindsey's peaceful face. "She's missed you all these years."

Suddenly, all that had happened back then seemed petty, and Tess began to feel guilty for not responding to Lindsey's pleas for forgiveness after Tess had found them in bed together. Now it was too late.

"I missed her, too."

Tess looked down at Johnny's hands, which were still holding hers, feeling the tables turning. It was Tess who now felt as though she were betraying a friend by holding the hands of Lindsey's husband while Lindsey rested in her coffin.

Tess pulled away... And Johnny lost control of his emotions.

She took him in her arms and held him close. She could feel Johnny's heart beating against her chest, could feel his warm breath graze her cheek as the low sob escaped him.

They didn't speak, nor did anyone approach them. Johnny's fellow officers, half of the Dawson Valley Police Force, lined the back wall of the funeral home, but showed no signs of intruding. Or maybe it was that they didn't dare get too close to Johnny's pain for fear of not knowing what to say, what to do.

Johnny sobbed like Tess had never heard before. It was a heartwrenching sound, causing a feeling of helplessness to rush through her body. If only there was something—anything—she could do to take away the pain.

There wasn't. Nobody could do anything for him. It was certain he would have the support of his friends and family. However, Johnny would have to endure this long road of anguish on his own because it was too soon for anything or anyone to lessen his pain.

"I'm sorry," he said, pulling away, once again maintaining composure.

"You can't keep this inside. If there's anything you need, I'm here for you." Tess didn't know how it would come across, but she wasn't able to help the words from coming out, didn't fully understood herself exactly what she meant by them.

"No, Tess... I am sorry."

It was time to go. Something about his repeated statement told her his words had nothing to do with Lindsey, and his wife's wake wasn't the time or the place to be letting such thoughts enter their minds.

Before she reached the comfort of the exit door, Johnny stopped her. He held her shoulders, only for a moment, holding her gaze through consoling eyes. After all the time apart, she still felt the tenderness in his touch, the way his fingers gently pressed into her skin, his heat radiating through the material of her silk blouse.

It was too much to bear. She stepped back, forcing Johnny to release his hold, enabling her to walk away from him and out into the open sunlight.

He followed.

"Tess."

She stopped and turned to face him. No words left her lips, only tears of regret uncontrollably poured down her face. He remained silent, his hands safely tucked in the pockets of his dress pants.

Tess continued to her car at the far end of the parking lot. It was safer this way. Sitting in her car, she glanced in the rearview mirror as Johnny stood there watching her.

Now Tess wondered why she had come here. Why had she come to see Johnny Sawyer, his wife's body lying in a coffin, his wife taken out of his life forever? Was it to see if she could do anything for him, to let him know she would be there if and when he needed her?

Tess tried to convince herself those were the reasons why

she sat staring at the funeral home but knew they weren't true. An unnerving chill ran through her body, giving her the answers to her questions.

Could I be that insensitive?

No...not intentionally.

Tess shook her head, then started the engine of her car, driving back down the tree-lined street, away from the man who had meant the world to her, the same man who had brought it crashing down.

She couldn't deal with the reemerging feelings, and they couldn't have come at a more disrespectful time. No. She didn't think she could ever confess to Johnny Sawyer how much she still loved him.

⚃

Johnny sat on the leather sectional, a pint of whiskey in hand, getting drunk out of his mind at ten o'clock in the morning on what would have seemed to anyone else an ordinary day.

Though she was gone, traces of Lindsey were still evident in the house. The furniture, the wall coverings, the vases full of silk flower arrangements...

She was everywhere.

So were the lies.

Lifting the half-empty bottle to his lips, Johnny took a long swig. He could feel the slow burn as the whiskey traveled down his throat to rest in the empty pit of his stomach. Everything seemed out of proportion, and he couldn't imagine waking up from this surreal nightmare any time soon.

Would he ever feel sane again?

During the last few months of Lindsey's life she had been intolerable to be around, fighting with him every chance she had. However, now, the whiskey almost gone, Johnny would have given anything to be able to relive the last day of her life.

To have her back.

He got up off the couch to use the bathroom, then promptly returned. Not having shaved in three days, he looked as though he'd been run over by a truck. Stronger than the lingering guilt over their final conversation was the image of Lindsey trapped in her car.

Johnny couldn't escape the haunting screams coming from the shadows of his mind...

When he'd heard the call go over the police scanner that night, the chance that it could've been his wife's car turned upside down on the curvy dirt road had never crossed his mind.

When he had arrived at the scene, his sergeant stepped out of a marked car about fifty yards from the accident and stopped him with the news that his wife was turned over in the ditch. Johnny jumped from the truck, wanting nothing more than to get to Lindsey.

One of the paramedics grabbed his arm, telling him she was already dead, but Johnny didn't believe it. As he scampered down the small hill, crawling to the car, a tow truck was turning the vehicle over from where it rested on its roof.

Johnny screamed for them not to move the car.

Out of respect, the crew stopped and ascended back up the hill to join the other onlookers, leaving Johnny with his grief. At the sight of the mangled sedan surrounding his wife, his grief forced the air from his lungs.

Johnny tried opening the door, but it wouldn't budge. He frantically ran around the car, climbing in through the passenger's side.

"Lindsey, baby, I'm here. You're going to be all right. Talk to me—say something—Lindsey!"

Johnny struggled to block the words *she's dead* out of his mind. Rubbing away the blood from her face, caressing her bruised cheek, he tried comforting her. But she didn't move.

Nothing helped.

Instinctively, Johnny touched two fingers to her wrist, checking for a pulse. None. He pressed his fingers to her neck— still nothing. Not even the wet blood on his face from placing his ear to her chest was enough to convince him she was truly gone.

"I'm getting you out of here. Hang on, baby...I'm going for help."

Johnny maneuvered his way out of the car, hurrying up the embankment, screaming in rage for someone—anyone—to save his wife. Everyone just stood, staring, eyes full of pity.

"What're you looking at? Get my wife to a hospital!" Johnny grabbed one of the paramedics by the shirt, savagely shaking him. "She needs help!"

"Detective Sawyer, she's gone. The impact of the crash was too much for her body to absorb," one of the officers informed him. "Let them do their job, and we'll get your wife out as soon as we can."

Johnny stood on the side of the road, his fists clenched in the paramedic's white shirt, trying to comprehend what was being said. He looked from his fists, to the officer, then up into the eyes of the man who had taken the brunt of Johnny's fury.

He loosened his hold on the paramedic but not before looking deep into his eyes. "Be careful with her, okay?"

"I will, Detective."

Johnny went back to his police cruiser and waited.

And watched…

He watched through tear-burning eyes as a second fire truck pulled up to the scene, eyeing the fireman as he descended the hill with the Jaws of Life. He cringed as they tore through the steel of Lindsey's car. Johnny fell apart when they finally pulled her lifeless body out of the vehicle, laying her on a gurney, covering her with a crisp white sheet.

It took all the power and strength he had to reach down and pull the handle to open the door of the cruiser. Filled with disbelief, Johnny approached the sheet-covered body.

"We'll give you some time alone, Detective."

Johnny waited for everyone to disperse. Little by little, he pulled back the sheet so he could see Lindsey's face. If it weren't for the blood smeared along her cheek, he'd have thought she was doing nothing more than taking a peaceful nap. But she was gone, and he wanted to know one thing.

Why?

"Why were you on this road?" he asked through grief-stricken emotion, stroking her dampened hair. "We talked on the phone an hour ago. What were you thinking?"

Then the pain and reality became too much to handle. The phone call, the argument about Johnny never being there for her.

If only he had been there…

Now it was too late.

Johnny leaned down, placing a soft kiss on Lindsey's lips, which were already cold to his touch, telling her he loved her. Then he pulled the sheet back over her face, motioning for the coroner to do his job.

He remembered people talking to him as he'd walked back to his police cruiser, but what they had said still wasn't clear.

The sound of his tires tearing through the dirt road had startled the crowd but hadn't made him falter on his journey out and away from the area that had taken his wife from him for good.

The hardest thing he'd had to do that night was drive to the house on Elmwood Parkway and tell Lindsey's parents that their only daughter was dead. Johnny never shed a tear. He knew if he had, he wouldn't have been able to stop. The last thing he had wanted was to be consoled.

The rest was a blank.

Even now. Johnny barely remembered going to the funeral home and making the arrangements. It was all still blurry. He wondered how he'd gotten this far. It had happened so fast—the accident, the wake, the funeral.

The sound of the doorbell pierced his ears. If there was one thing he didn't need, it was company. It would only be more sympathetic words. *You're going to make it through this; life works in mysterious ways; these things happen for a reason.*

He had heard them all.

"Not again today," he sighed.

Sitting in silence, trying to ignore the door, didn't work. Instead of pushing the button, his visitor now used knuckles, rapping obnoxiously, continuously. Johnny picked up the whiskey bottle, pulling his arm back as if to throw it against the wall, then withdrew. His actions would only accomplish a floor full of shattered glass.

His life was shattered enough.

Taking his time getting up off the couch, Johnny wiped his eyes with the heels of his hands, stretched his back then looked at the door. The knocking continued along with the familiar hollering of his partner.

"I know you're in there, man. Open up," Mike Foster yelled

from the front porch.

He would rather be left alone but knew Mike wasn't going to give up. He opened the front door, immediately turning his back on Mike as he walked to the couch.

"Took you long enough to answer." Mike came in and shut the door. "Did I wake you up?"

"Do I look like I've been sleeping?"

"You look like hell." Mike sat in the leather recliner, gazing from the whiskey bottle to Johnny. "I know what you're going through has to seem like you're dying, too, but you're not." He gave Johnny a solid stare. "It's awful what happened to Lindsey, and you should take all the time you need to grieve. But, Johnny, you can't let yourself fall into that bottle."

"You have no idea what I'm going through. Last time I knew, you didn't have a wife."

"I'm on your side. Just calm—"

"For God's sake, at thirty years old, you're still out trying to tag every piece of ass you can get your hands on! Don't sit there and tell me that you know what I'm going through."

Johnny got up, went to the dining room and opened the door of the liquor cabinet. He pulled out a fresh bottle of whiskey and brought two glasses to the table. Mike shook his head, declining the offer of a morning drink.

"I'm sorry, man. I want to help you." Mike watched as Johnny took a mouthful of the brown liquid straight from the bottle before filling his glass.

"No one can help. I need to handle this on my own."

"Is that what you told Tess?"

"What the hell does she have to do with this?" Johnny leaned back on the couch, bringing the whiskey to his lips while peering over the rim of the glass.

"I saw you two at the funeral home. Everyone did."

"What's your point?"

"What was she doing there?"

Johnny glared at Mike. "Is it so wrong that she came to pay her last respects to Lindsey?"

"Let's be honest, Johnny. Did she come for Lindsey? Or for you?"

"I can't believe you're giving me hell about Tess. You know they used to be friends."

"Yeah, before Tess found you in bed with her best friend," Mike said.

"That was years ago. I'm glad Tess came. It would've meant a lot to Lindsey."

"It makes me wonder..."

"What the hell are you talking about?"

"Let me ask you this." Mike leaned forward, elbows resting on his knees. "How did it make you feel to see her? You got pretty emotional in her arms."

"I'm not going to talk about this. My wife just died, and you're dwelling on a girl I dated eleven years ago!"

"A girl you dated? Is that how you saw your relationship with Tess? I think she'd be offended by that."

"Damn it, Mike, what the hell are you getting at?"

"Since you're not going to tell me, I'll ask."

"By all means." Johnny continued knocking back the glass of whiskey.

"What was Tess doing here this morning?" Mike finally got Johnny's attention. "I came by earlier and saw her car sitting across the street. Granted she was in it, but I'm sure sooner or later she came to the door."

"You're the only person who's been here banging on my door. I think you were seeing things."

"I wasn't seeing things, my friend. It was Tess, not wasting one moment to come back to you. Now, of all times."

"If Tess was out there, and I stress *if*, she didn't come to the door. Yesterday was the first time I've talked to her in years."

Johnny knew what Mike was getting at but also knew Tess hadn't had any ulterior motives when coming to the funeral home. She wasn't the type of person to use a situation like this to her advantage.

Mike and Johnny had been best friends since their football days in high school. They had played all the same sports, got into all kinds of adolescent trouble together and even fought over a girl from time to time.

Tess Fenmore having been their biggest fight ever.

Mike and Johnny had argued plenty about Tess. Mike's excuse had been that he didn't like her, thought she was a stuck-up snob. Except Johnny knew his best friend all too well. Although Mike had never admitted it, Johnny knew he'd had a thing for Tess back then.

"All I'm saying is you've got enough to deal with right now, and the last thing you need is Tess Fenmore hanging around, messing you up all over again." Mike stood.

"How are things at the station?" Johnny asked, changing a subject neither of them had ever agreed on. "Have they found out anything more about the accident?"

"We've determined by the tire marks that there wasn't another vehicle involved. It was just that, Johnny, a tragic accident."

"How can you be so sure?" he demanded. He wanted

someone to blame, wanted to ease his guilt.

"You know how we determine between an accident and a homicide, Johnny. We played everything by the book."

"I'll never understand why Lindsey went out in that storm." Johnny took another drink, then set the glass on the coffee table. "Why was she headed out that way of all places? You know how bad that road can be at night."

"I know."

Johnny's gaze dropped, the guilt again washing over him. "If this counseling session is over, I want to take a shower."

"I don't want you to worry about work. We've got things covered. Take all the time you need." Mike started for the door. "Try to keep out of the bottle. That whisky will only make things worse."

"How much worse can they get?"

"Trust me," Mike stressed. "A lot."

With that said, he was gone.

"Worse my ass!" Johnny screamed, this time throwing the glass across the suffocating room, smashing the picture on the mantle in the process. "Oh, dear God…"

He went to the fireplace, then knelt to gather the picture, carefully swiping away the shards of glass from the faces staring back at him. The faces of a couple who had once been happy, one of them still here, the other gone, taking with her the secrets that had destroyed their marriage long before her death had.

Leaving the mess behind, Johnny started for the stairs but couldn't manage to make his way up. To go up would mean he would have to enter their bedroom.

He couldn't face what was waiting for him in there.

The smell of her perfume still lingered in the room, her silk robe covered the back of the chair in front of her vanity. Worst of all, the pregnancy test she had taken the last day he'd seen her alive was still on the counter in the bathroom.

If he hadn't felt bad enough that his wife was dead, it killed him to find out she'd been pregnant, too. Maybe that's why she'd wanted him to come home so badly that day, to tell him the good news that they had accepted over the years would never come.

He couldn't figure it out.

Her mood had been foul toward him. Why hadn't she come busting through the station doors with the little white strip of plastic in her hand? They had waited a long time for something like that.

Again, the sound of the doorbell echoed throughout the house. Johnny stood and went to the door, throwing it open.

"Damn it, Mike, I thought we were—"

But it wasn't Mike.

"Hello, Johnny."

"Jennings, what the hell are you doing here?"

Although they'd both grown up in Dawson Valley, Ted Jennings was more of an acquaintance than a friend, and the fact that he was the shrink for Internal Affairs made him the last person Johnny wanted to deal with.

"I thought I could lend you an ear." Ted stepped through the door without Johnny's invite. "Off the record."

"What's going on in my life doesn't involve my job." Johnny kicked the door fully open, waiting for Ted to take the hint. "We have nothing to talk about."

"I didn't come here for the sake of business." Ted took a seat on the couch, lifted the whiskey bottle to his nose, then set it back down. "Don't you think it's a bit early?"

"I don't remember asking for your opinion." Johnny slammed the door shut and moved into the room. "If you don't mind, I was in the middle of something."

"I can see that." Ted looked at the floor where Johnny had thrown the glass, to the picture that still rested there, shattered within its frame. "I lost my wife two years ago to a drunk driver. Never thought I'd get through it."

Ted's assertion was unexpected, making Johnny feel like a jerk for being rude.

"I'm sorry," Johnny said flatly, kneeling down, picking up the larger pieces of glass, in no position to be consoling someone else. "How the hell did you do it?"

"What?"

"Drag yourself out of bed in the morning?" Johnny set the glass on the brick hearth of the fireplace, then sat on the floor facing the couch.

"I know you don't want to hear this, but it takes time. The emptiness will never go away, but the pain...it subsides."

"And the guilt?" Johnny stared at the bottle of whiskey. "Does that ever go away?"

"What is it you feel guilty about?"

"Did the Chief send you here?" Johnny felt his body tense.

"I told you my visit has nothing to do with business."

"Then why are you starting to sound like a shrink by answering my question with a question?"

"Look..." Ted stood. "I thought maybe it would help for you to talk, but I can see coming here was a mistake. Too soon... If you ever need to talk, you know where to find me."

He got all the way to the door before something in Johnny reached out to stop him.

"Lindsey and I argued the night she died. She called me at

25

the station, and I let her have it." Ted slowly turned around, listening. "For the last year I had a hard time coping with Lindsey. Whether it was something she was going through, I don't know, but her moods had become intolerable."

Ted came back into the living room and again took his seat on the couch. "What'd you argue about?"

"She said she was sick of being home alone, accused me of never being there for her." Johnny looked at Ted.

"Was there any truth to that?"

"I started working a lot of hours. She accused me of having an affair."

"Were you?" Ted asked.

"Hell no!" Johnny waited for Ted to shoot another question his way, but he didn't. "That was always her way of avoiding the real problems in our marriage. Damn it, I'd had it, told her that once and for all we were going to lay everything out on the table. That she was going to open up so we could get through our problems."

"And did she?"

"We never had the chance. She hung up that night, and that's the last time we talked." Johnny stood and went to the fireplace, looking at each photo as he approached. "Hanging up was a habit of hers, so it didn't surprised me." He quickly turned to face Ted. "If I had thought she'd jump in her car and go out in that storm..." He ran his fingers through his hair. "I wish I would have gone home."

"You couldn't have known." Ted shook his head. "I see why you feel guilty, though. Like I said, I've been there."

"I guess the question is, Doc, where do I go from here? How do I move on?"

"As hard as it sounds, you need to let go. The pain, the

guilt, you need to let it all go because, bottom line, this tragedy was not your fault. Until you accept that, you'll never be able to heal and move on." Ted got up and walked to the door, turning back to leave Johnny with one last piece of advice. "Just be careful how you do it."

"What do you mean?"

"Tess Fenmore." Ted held up his hands to silence Johnny. "Although we never ran in the same circles growing up, I remember you two were an item for quite some time. I don't know why things didn't work between you two, why you ended up marrying her best friend, but yesterday, the look in your eyes when you saw her... It's clear that you still have unresolved issues with Tess. I hope you know what you're doing, Johnny."

Not waiting for a response, Ted left.

Johnny got up and went out to the enclosed backyard. This house had too many memories to deal with. Sad to say, Ted had been right. They all started with Tess. Johnny should've never bought this house and tried to make a life there with another woman.

That had been his first and biggest mistake.

It had been less than twenty-four hours since he had buried his wife, yet Johnny couldn't take it any more. As soon as he collected his bearings long enough to pick up the phone and call the real-estate agent, he would. He was going to pack everything up and move. There was no way he could go on with his life in a house full of memories and hidden secrets of the past.

Looking out to the makeshift pond in the center of the yard, Johnny thought back to his conversation with Mike. Was Mike just being himself by making more out of Tess's sudden reappearance in Johnny's life? Or was there some truth to what he had said? If Tess had come to his house that morning, she certainly hadn't come to the door.

What would he have done if she had? Slam it in her face like he had wanted to do to Mike and Ted Jennings? Or would he have given in to the unthinkable, taking her again into his arms and never letting her go, desperately holding onto the possibility that she could make all the pain go away?

Through the agonizing throbbing in his head, Johnny asked himself how any man could think about another woman when his wife had been laid to rest merely the day before?

What made the pain more excruciating was that the disturbing thoughts wouldn't go away. They were still there, tearing, pulling at his soul.

Chapter Two

A week had gone by since Lindsey's funeral and only a few days since Tess had phoned Lindsey's parents with condolences. She'd hoped to do so at the wake, but they'd been surrounded by family and she hadn't wanted to intrude. When she spoke to Mrs. Moran, it broke Tess's heart to hear the sadness in her voice, the pain of losing her daughter, and the hurt that Lindsey's brother Luke hadn't shown up to say goodbye to his sister, to be there for his parents.

Now, Tess looked through the gate of the Lake Crest Cemetery. Nestled amongst the hundred-year-old maple trees were mausoleums of the rich, stationed in the center, away from the bordering wrought-iron fence. Decrepit flat stones were spread throughout the graveyard with names and dates barely visible due to the elements of nature.

Tess parked her car in the semicircular driveway in front of the cemetery's information center, then entered the graveyard. If the sun hadn't been out in full she would have driven in. The newer section was a good half mile down the paved lane. But today, she needed desperately to clear her head, and, with any luck, the walk would help.

Lindsey was buried in this cemetery. As for where, that was to be determined, and the newer section was the best place to start looking.

Tess stopped midway, turning back to her car.

"What am I doing here?" she said to the emptiness around her. "What could possibly come from me being here?"

All the same, she continued on her way into the cemetery, determined to find what she was looking for. Every time she spotted a dirt rectangle in the midst of the lush grass, she stopped to look. Some of the plots already had cemented headstones. Others did not.

What if Lindsey's grave hadn't been completed with a stone yet? Tess looked around to see if there were any more nearby clearings. About three sections down the lane she noticed one.

When she reached the spot, Tess stood, the back of the stone facing her. She wasn't able to divert her gaze from the fresh soil. With an overwhelming feeling that she had found the grave she was looking for, Tess slowly walked around the dirt perimeter to read the rose-colored stone, a chill taking over her body.

Carved along the front of the rounded granite top read: *Rest In Peace.* Written from one side to the next, in three even rows, read: *Lindsey Moran Sawyer; Loving Wife And Daughter; 1974-2008.* It was simple yet skillfully engraved within the rock.

No matter how many years had gone by since Johnny and Lindsey had married, it seemed strange when faced with the name. Lindsey Sawyer. Tess took the fresh tulips she'd brought, their color the lightest lavender, and placed them in front of the stone.

It saddened her to think back on Lindsey lying in the coffin, now buried six feet below the newly turned-up space.

How do people move on from such tragedy?

Tess had never lost someone close to her. Though the love lost between her and her once best friend hadn't been great, it was still hard to face. If Tess was feeling such immense emptiness, she couldn't imagine how Lindsey's parents and Johnny were dealing with her death.

"Funny finding you here. Although, I'm not surprised."

Tess turned her head. She hadn't been aware that anyone had seen her. When she saw the man who'd made such a frank comment, she realized she should have known who it was without having to look.

If not for Johnny, Tess wouldn't have ever associated with Mike Foster. In his youth, Mike had trouble written all over his face. Now as an adult, he still did.

"Don't you have anything to say?" He took a pack of cigarettes from his shirt pocket, lit one up then took a long drag, as if contemplating his next jab at Tess. "Seems you've been getting around since things went south." He nodded toward Lindsey's grave.

"You're still the same inconsiderate bastard you've always been." Tess stood, wiping away the tears that had trickled down her cheek. "I hardly call going to Lindsey's wake and coming here getting around."

"My, my, still such animosity." Mike smirked. "What do you think Lindsey would say if she knew you were curbside to her house the other day, determining how best to go about getting her husband back?"

"How dare you imply that that's what I was doing?" Tess took a step toward Mike. "What, Detective...got nothing better to do than trail me?"

"Someone has to make sure Johnny doesn't do anything stupid again. God knows anything's possible in his state of mind." Mike crushed the butt of the half-smoked cigarette beneath his black shoe.

"Not that I owe you an explanation, but I would never take advantage of Johnny at a time like this."

"At a time like this?" Mike mocked her words. "His wife's body isn't even cold yet, and here you are putting yourself back into his life after all these—"

"That's enough!"

Tess jumped at the sharpness of the male voice. Running up the lane was Johnny. She hadn't seen him approaching and by the look on Mike's face, neither had he. An unmistakable feeling of intrusion again came over her.

"Don't you dare do this here!" Johnny hissed at his partner through clenched teeth, giving Tess a sideward glance.

"I'm sorry you had to hear that," Mike acknowledged, as if he'd been trying to do Johnny a huge service by degrading Tess alongside Lindsey's grave.

"It's better if I go." Tess looked at Johnny. "I'm sorry. I overstepped by coming here."

She started retracing her steps through the manicured setting to the shelter of her car. She thought she'd be able to leave in silence, without further confrontation, but Johnny's voice demanded her to stop.

"Wait! I want to talk to you."

"This should be good." Mike reached for another cigarette with no regard for either of their feelings.

"Leave," Johnny said, halting him.

For a moment, Mike looked at Tess, at Johnny, then shook his head, throwing his hands in the air.

"Whatever you say, Johnny. Just remember what I told you." Mike glared at Tess, pointing a stiff finger. "And you, don't forget... I know what you're up to."

Tess didn't respond, didn't wander back to Lindsey's graveside, rather waited for Johnny to make the next move.

"Damn it, Mike, get the hell out of here!"

After Mike left, Johnny moved in Tess's direction, his head bowed.

Tess felt more uncomfortable than she ever had. If only she had listened to her inner voice and gone back to her car. But no, she had come to this very spot and been thrown into an argument. It reminded her of when they were kids, and seeing Johnny at the cemetery wasn't something she had planned on.

When he reached her, underneath the tall red maple tree, he stopped, lifting his head. The grief in his eyes was immense. She wasn't sure how to handle him. Johnny had prevented her from leaving, so Tess waited for him to speak first.

"I'm sorry about that." Johnny nodded toward the empty path that Mike had taken when leaving the cemetery.

"I can handle Mike."

"You always could, couldn't you?"

For a brief moment, Johnny's face held the comings of a smile. Tess wanted to run to him, to absorb all of his pain, but knew that wasn't realistic. How had they ever gotten to this point?

She should have found a way to forgive him and Lindsey for what they had done, and tried to move forward as friends. Tess had had no choice but to accept them as a married couple.

Her biggest mistake had been never looking back. If only they could have worked things out, the three of them, Tess would have been able to help Johnny now without people thinking she had a hidden agenda.

"I didn't think anyone would be here." Tess put her hands in the pockets of her jeans. "Speaking of which, I'll let you be alone."

"Don't... That's my problem. The only welcomed company I've had lately is the comfort of a whiskey bottle, and all it's managed to do is give me one hell of a headache."

"That seems to be how it works." Although Tess wasn't much of a drinker, she understood Johnny finding such solitary comfort.

"Why do I feel so guilty?" Johnny asked.

"About what?"

"Talking to you...here."

"I know what you mean." Tess closed her eyes, holding back the tears, reopening them only when her emotions were under control. "That's why I should go."

"No, you shouldn't. No matter what happened, she was *your* friend."

Was he trying to convince her of that or himself?

"She was... Once upon a time." Tess walked back over to the grave and knelt down.

She took the flowers, rearranging them so they fanned out in front of the headstone. She watched the shadow of Johnny approaching her side but didn't dare look up.

The whole setting was bizarre, and she didn't know how to deal with it. Something had brought her to his house the other day, but she had never made it to his door for fear of not knowing what to say, not sure what would be accomplished from her visit.

The words didn't come any easier now.

"Tulips were always her favorite." Johnny knelt down beside Tess. "I haven't been able to bring myself to come back here until today."

Tess looked at him with regret.

"I'm sure the last thing you expected was to find Mike and me at each other's throats."

"I know it had nothing to do with you." He sat on the damp ground. "What do you think it means?"

"What?"

"Finding you here."

"I don't know. It's so strange. I still can't believe this has happened."

She wasn't ready to give in to fate as an explanation, and she wasn't sure she could believe it had anything to do with destiny at all.

"I'm still waiting to wake up. It's like being trapped inside a horrifying nightmare...the way the world continues to go on around me." Johnny tried to rub the stress from his face but only caused himself apparent irritation. "Damn it! If only I knew why she had gone out there that night, maybe I could make some sense of this."

"There's no way you can." Tess stood, then walked away from the grave so she could see his face. "You can't keep beating yourself up. Johnny, you need to let yourself grieve the loss of your wife. Whatever was going through Lindsey's mind that night, you'll never know."

"If only it were that simple."

"I know it's not, but what more can you do?" She tried not to sound insensitive.

"If only you knew." He, too, stood and started to leave.

"Knew what?" Tess called after him as she began to follow.

"Nothing. Just let it go, all right?"

He showed no signs of stopping, and she didn't want to push. She stood, watching Johnny depart. It wasn't until he was out of sight that she went back to Lindsey's grave.

"What was he talking about?" She asked for an answer that would never grace her ears.

Not from the ground, anyway.

If she had helped him today, just a little, that would be enough for her. She wanted badly to be there for Johnny. He had taken the time to talk to her, but it was obvious he hadn't wanted to let her in.

And really, why should he?

Tess looked once more to the gravesite, to the spot she would like to think was no more than a place for those left behind to visit. Lindsey was now in another world, a better place, a utopia. One day Tess believed she would again see her friend, and the problems they had had in this lifetime would be meaningless in the next.

C3

Johnny never left the cemetery but walked far enough away so he could watch Tess. Being there with her made him feel as though he were deceiving the memory of Lindsey. Yet earlier when she had started to walk away, something in Johnny had screamed out to stop her.

His sudden call out for her to stay had to do with not wanting to leave his thoughts unsaid. He had made that mistake too many times in his life. In spite of everything, that's why he was feeling guilty for the way he had left things with Lindsey on the phone the night she died.

Though it hadn't been Johnny who hung up the phone, looking back, he should have left the station immediately and gone straight home. But it hadn't been the first time his wife had been that upset with him. Like all the times before, he'd thought the argument could wait until he got home.

Now the mistake could never be undone.

After Tess had departed, Johnny went back and kneeled

before the headstone. He had never been one to believe in visiting a cemetery, an empty place...

A place where the living supposedly returned for comfort. Johnny was feeling no type of comfort. All it did was remind him Lindsey was gone. Gone forever. Yet he had still come. He wasn't sure what he was looking for. Perhaps some answers, a sign that it was okay to go on with his life, undeniably something he would have to do.

He'd started taking a step in that direction by putting his house on the market. The realtor had brought over a couple of prospective buyers that morning. That's why Johnny had left the house. He couldn't bring himself to be *that* close to letting go.

Packing up Lindsey's belongings had given Johnny time to go over the life they'd had together. Now that everything was black and white, he was forced to admit that most of it hadn't been happy at all.

They'd had their share of good times, like most estranged marriages had had at one point or another. But, from Johnny's perspective, none of it had been built on an undying love, rather a way to get over another person. Tess Fenmore.

Could Lindsey hear his thoughts? He had to believe she would understand, although it no longer mattered. However, it would matter to the people who were left behind. For them, especially Lindsey's parents, to know that he was thinking of another woman would be impossible for them to comprehend.

At one point in his life, Tess had meant the world to him. No matter his reasoning for ending things, Tess had taken a huge part of him with her when she had left. The place Johnny always had for her in his heart had never been filled by anyone else—not even Lindsey—nor did he think it could ever be.

If circumstances were different, he wouldn't think twice

about going to Tess, telling her that he'd never stopped loving her. Perhaps with him being emotionally messed up at the moment, she would only think it was his way of rebounding, avoiding a loss he was being forced to face.

Johnny reached down, picking up one of the tulips. He asked for Lindsey's forgiveness, vowing never to come back to the cemetery, to the reality of what his life had become. Dead.

Standing, then turning away, he left with the comfort of the one tulip he still held. Maybe somehow it could help him move on, toward the woman he had pushed away many years ago.

All the same, for the time being, he couldn't do anything. He felt nothing but contempt for himself for feeling this way. He didn't know how his heart could be trying to heal with only the thoughts of Tess helping it along.

He looked up to the sky. There was no use thinking about Tess any more. Standing back and accepting that he'd fallen out of love with Lindsey a long time ago was too hard to deal with now that she was gone, leaving him with nothing more than a whole lot of guilt.

03

Tess desperately needed someone to talk to. At a time like this, a loving, nonjudgmental mother would have come in real handy.

If only I had one.

But she had always had her father. They had made a pact long ago to get together every week for lunch, except the last few weeks, Tess had let herself become withdrawn from him, too.

Her dad had called every night since Lindsey died, checking in to see how she was doing, and seemed to understand Tess's need for space by not asking any questions. Up until now, she hadn't felt a strong need to open up to anyone.

She pulled into an old warehouse parking lot, then turned around. If she hurried, she would still be able to catch him before he left. Knowing her luck, she would miss her dad the day she needed him the most.

She drove up to the curb of her father's office building. He worked for the city as the chief inspector for the development bureau. Any time a new building went up in town, her father was the one who went to make sure everything was up to code.

He loved what he did, and he was great at it. When Tess had been looking for her first home, her dad had been right by her side, making sure she wasn't investing her hard-earned wages into a money pit. He had shown her a lot of well-built homes, but none of them had appealed.

Driving home from work one day, she had found her dream house. From the first moment she laid eyes on the Cape Cod-style home, Tess had fallen in love with it. However, her dad hadn't been concerned with what the outside looked like. It had been in his nature to make sure the inside lived up to its contemporary good looks.

After putting a few coins in the parking meter, Tess walked through the front door and up the stairs to the main offices, where everyone greeted her with the usual *hellos.*

She had been to her dad's office many times throughout the years. It was the only place she could go to see him. There were a few occasions when Tess had mustered up the strength to go to her parents' house, but it was something she tended to avoid.

She still dreaded being anywhere near her mother.

When Tess approached the open door of his office, she could hear her dad on the phone. She waited until he finished his call before walking through the door.

"What a pleasant surprise," Eric Fenmore said.

"Hi, Dad." Tess gave him a hug, then dropped into the leather chair in front of his desk.

"Were we supposed to have lunch today?" He finished putting some loose papers into a black folder, then turned his full attention to her.

"No, I just thought I'd stop by and see what you've been up to."

"What's wrong?" he asked. "I'm betting this isn't a social call."

"I'm sorry I've been so distant lately. So much is going on, and I didn't know where to turn."

"So you found yourself here." He smiled.

Tess nodded.

"I'm glad you felt you could come to me." He got up, taking the seat next to her.

"You're the only one I could turn to." Tess propped her feet up on the desk in front of her, drooping down farther in the chair. "How'd you know something was wrong?"

"You've always been so strong, but I'd be a fool not to notice something is eating away at you. I could tell that much by our phone conversations. However, I didn't want to pry."

"I appreciate that." Tess smiled.

"Now that you're here, why don't you tell me what's on your mind." He got up to fetch the two of them a cup of coffee. "If you're ready to talk."

Tess told him about everything. Lindsey's wake, sitting out in front of Johnny's house, then her run-in with Mike and Johnny at the cemetery. She expressed to her dad the confusion she had over Johnny's comment at the funeral home about being sorry, but the one thing she had a hard time telling him was something he already knew.

"After all these years you still love Johnny Sawyer, don't you?"

"I thought I'd gotten over that part of my life. I mean, I *did*, everything that happened and all." She sighed. "Until recently, I didn't realize how much I still love him." She looked to her dad for sympathy. "Is that awful or what?"

"That you love him?"

"No...the timing. He just lost his wife—someone who used to mean a lot to me, too—and all I can think about is him...us."

"You're only human, Tess. We can't control our feelings." He set his coffee cup down, taking her hand. "I'm not going to sugarcoat it. These reoccurring feelings are going to put you on an emotional roller coaster."

"I know, they already are." Tess got up, walking to the window overlooking the business district of Dawson Valley. "That's what's driving me mad."

"Has Johnny said something more specific pertaining to how he feels?"

"No, but you should've seen his face when he told me he was sorry. He stressed it, making me feel as though it was about us...not Lindsey. Do you know where I'm coming from? What would he have to be sorry for to *me* about his wife?"

"Slow down and take a breath." Her dad walked over to stand next to her. "What happened next?"

"I didn't give him the chance to explain, but I knew what he meant."

"What was that?" her father asked.

"Dad, I never told you what happened after Johnny and I broke up."

"I know it hurt you when he got together with Lindsey, and the whole unfortunate mess damaged your relationship with her, too."

"It did. The truth is, I walked in on them in bed together. It was months after Johnny and I split up, but it still killed me inside." She smoothed her forehead with cold fingertips, trying to rid herself of all thoughts.

"I don't know where to begin with this. I've always liked Johnny. You know that. But Tess, I think you really need to let him come to you."

"I know what you're going to say, and I don't want to be some diversion to help him get over this tragedy."

"I'm glad you understand that," he said.

"It doesn't make things any clearer."

"I'm not saying Johnny doesn't have feelings for you, but losing Lindsey only makes the situation more complicated."

"Don't I know it."

"Give it some time, see what happens."

She felt better finally talking to someone about Johnny. However, her mind was still rambling with the same thoughts as before. Her dad was right about one thing. She needed to let Johnny be the one to come to her. The only problem was she had a hard time waiting for someone else to make the first move.

For now, all she could do was promise herself she'd take things day by day. *Who are you trying to fool?* she questioned her good sense. She was too set in her life, too strong-minded, to wait around for someone to throw her a curveball.

She needed answers.

She would bet her life there was more going on with Johnny than he was willing to admit. The question was—would she have the nerve to ask him *what?*

More importantly, would she be able to accept his explanation?

Chapter Three

When the last box left the house and was loaded into the moving van, only then did Johnny pull the pregnancy test from his pocket. Along with the memories within the house, he needed to leave this behind, too. There wasn't anyone on earth who could bring his wife or the baby back.

It had been six months since Lindsey died. He had finally sold the house and bought a small farmhouse outside the city. Though the pain was still there, stronger than ever, time didn't stand still.

He had to move on. For his own sanity, he needed to get away from the past before he went mad. He vowed not to bring all the doubts and regrets to his new home.

That had been the whole point of moving in the first place.

He had managed to keep to himself, and only at work did he allow for any extra interaction with people. Although Lindsey's parents continued to invite him over on Sundays for family dinner, Johnny politely declined. Every time. All he wanted was to be left alone.

And alone he was.

He had never felt so alone in his whole life. It was as though the world around him didn't exist any more. He went on day by day with his routine, but he was merely going through the motions. The only time he had any wits about him was on the job.

Being a detective called for his undivided attention, and he'd always given it his all. The job was his rock. It gave him eight to ten hours out of the day when he didn't have to think about his emotional nonexistence. Without it, he would've fallen completely apart.

He went from room to room, making sure he hadn't left anything behind in the old house. Not a material thing was in sight, only memories of another lifetime. That's how everything seemed to him now. Far away, yet close enough to still haunt him.

Johnny took one last look, then closed the door, vowing to leave it all behind.

He gave the same inspection as he circled the outside of the house, looking for anything that needed to be thrown out or for something worthwhile enough to be put in the back of his SUV. But he should have known there hadn't been anything left. He had already meticulously taken care of everything the first time around.

That had been hard enough.

Before walking back to the front of the house, Johnny held out the plastic strip before him. It was like looking down at the ghost of someone he would never know, reminding him of Lindsey's deceit for not telling him sooner... If there was anything he'd realized since losing his wife, it was how much of a stranger she had become to him during the last few years.

Johnny walked around to the back of the garage, the familiar stress suffocating him, then lifted the lid of the metal trash can. The sound of the plastic hitting the empty bottom rang loud through the otherwise-quiet afternoon, bouncing lies upon lies off the inner walls of his mind, causing him to look down into the dark can.

That was his last tie to this chapter in his life. It was all over. He had rid himself of the proof...proof of a child, proof of a family, but more importantly, proof of the undying secrets of a woman he'd thought he loved.

Johnny replaced the lid then proceeded back around to the driveway and got in his vehicle. It was time for him to wake up to the world, to the existence around him, before life swallowed him whole. He had been a prisoner in his own shell for some time now, yet he still wasn't able to make sense out of any of it.

He couldn't wait to get up tomorrow and go to the station. With each passing day, he had begun to look forward to work. The feeling wasn't altogether new to him. That's how he had felt for the last two years living with Lindsey and the destruction that had become their marriage.

When he drove away from the house, he rolled the windows down on both sides of the SUV, letting the air rush in to clear his senses. From the time when Lindsey died, he had kept himself completely closed up to everything around him.

It wasn't going to be easy, but he knew it was time. Time to move on and out of this neighborhood. Away from the house, the street and a life that no longer existed. Johnny shifted into high gear and drove to his new farmhouse.

However, no matter how hard he tried to forget, he knew the old memories would haunt him there, too.

ങ

With the last word to the file typed, it was time to go home. Tess had been so enthralled with working on the numerous depositions that she hadn't realized the afternoon had blown by. Keeping herself busy didn't leave time for concentrating on the here and now.

The day she had run into Johnny at the cemetery seemed as though it had been yesterday. Although pinpointing the date proved it to have been many months ago. Working for the law firm adjacent to the police station, Tess had hoped she would spot Johnny on his way into work. She had spotted his SUV in the parking lot at the end of every day, but never once had she caught a glimpse of him.

Maybe Johnny didn't want to see her. If he did, he knew where to find her. For that reason, she hadn't pursued him. Not a single phone call or a question to one of his fellow officers inquiring as to how he was doing.

Tess got up, stretching her back, massaging her neck muscles. Sometimes the days seemed to drag. But today hadn't, and she couldn't wait to go home, get out of her black pinstriped suit and take the bobby pins out of her hair. A soak in a hot bath was what she needed, but thoughts of Johnny Sawyer were sure to reemerge the second her body relaxed.

It was the end of the workweek, and the weekends were always the worst. Trying to keep her mind busy seemed to be such a chore these days. On many occasions she'd had friends over or gone out for a late dinner date or two, but most of the time she was forced to entertain herself.

She turned off the computer then locked the filing cabinets on her way to the door. After shutting off the lights, she headed down the hall to the elevator. She stepped in, but as the door started to close an arm stopped it from sliding shut.

"Hey there."

Tess forced a smile, fumbling with the leather strap of her purse.

"If you won't let me take you out, the least you could do is hold the door for me," Rex Cramer said, pushing his way into the elevator.

"I didn't see you coming."

Rex was a junior partner in the law firm. Seeing as his name hadn't yet been engraved on the door, Tess was sure his position was still debatable. He had been bugging her to go out ever since the day he had started there. Tess wasn't interested. His arrogant personality had a way of surpassing his good looks.

"That's what you always say." He gave her a questioning look then rolled his eyes, mocking her tone. *"I didn't see you coming."*

To avoid further hassles, Tess forced a smile, willing the elevator to move faster.

When they reached the main level, the door slid open and Tess wasted no time stepping out, not giving Rex any further consideration. Though, as always, she knew he wouldn't let her get away without trying to gain her attention.

The vivid sunlight was a welcome relief from the stuffy office and closed quarters of the elevator. Tess couldn't remember the weather being this nice when she had taken respite at the picnic table for lunch. Looking at her car, she hoped Rex would take the direction to his own.

No such luck.

"Why don't you go out with me tonight?" He stopped next to her car. "We could check out that new Italian restaurant over on Central Boulevard. I heard the atmosphere is kickin'."

"Tonight won't work for me." Tess dug out her keys then pressed the keypad, unlocking her car door, waiting with patience for Rex to step back. "I have plans, but maybe some other time."

"Where have I heard that before?" He leaned an elbow on

the hood of her car. "I bet if you wanted to, you could rearrange your plans."

"Really, I can't—"

"Come on..." Rex reached over, lightly caressing her arm. "Sure you can."

"Is there a problem here?"

At first, the sound of his voice stunned her. But when Tess glanced over her shoulder and saw Johnny, she couldn't have been happier. Happy to finally see him again and happy that she had kept a promise to herself, as hard as it had been, taking her father's advice by letting *him* come to her even if his sudden appearance had most likely been by coincidence.

"Just trying to talk the lady into having dinner with me." Rex removed his hand from Tess's arm.

"How long have you known Tess?" Johnny asked.

"Long enough to think there wouldn't be any harm in the two of us sharing an evening together." Rex winked at Tess.

"If you knew her as well as you think you do, you'd know Tess doesn't persuade easily."

A small chuckle rolled past her lips.

"Who said I had to persuade her?" Rex shot Johnny a look filled with irritation, then focused again on Tess. "So, what do you say?"

"Not tonight, maybe another time."

"You can't blame a guy for trying." He shrugged, keeping his pride intact. "I guess I'll see you Monday."

Rex bowed out to Tess, then went on his way, but not before giving Johnny one last glare.

Tess threw her purse on the front seat, butterflies invading her stomach, then turned to face Johnny. It was a welcome surprise seeing him but still very much a surprise.

"That guy's an asshole," he commented, watching as Rex climbed into his car.

"He's harmless."

"He's still an asshole." Johnny swatted a fly from the sleeve of his shirt.

"How are you?"

"You weren't really going to go out with him, were you?" Johnny replied instead of answering her question.

"Are you kidding me? I was seconds away from having to get downright rude with the man." She took a small comfort in Johnny's protectiveness.

"Some people can't take a hint...the poor sap."

"How've you been?" Tess repeated.

"I'm still breathing, so I guess that says something."

"I'm glad to hear that."

For a moment they both stood in silence. Johnny loosened his tie, unbuttoned the neck of his shirt. Tess assumed he was just getting off duty, probably dreading the drive to his empty house.

"So..." she said.

"So."

Their small talk was only taking them so far.

"Are you done for the day?"

"If you can say that. I'm always on call." Johnny smiled, tapping the beeper connected to his waistband, nodding toward the police station.

That smile...

She remembered the way he used to look at her. The evident dimple on the left side of his face had always sent chills through her body. Although they weren't kids any more,

Johnny's smile still had the same effect.

"Do you really have plans tonight?" he asked.

"Depends."

"What kind of answer's that?"

"It depends on who's asking."

"I bet that would really piss Cramer off." He laughed.

"Are you making me an offer?"

"What if I was?" Johnny took a step closer. "Would you tell me that you already have plans, too?"

"I've always been one to weigh my options."

"That's good to know." Johnny kicked around the loose gravel as if contemplating his next response. "Do you want to have dinner with me?"

"There *is* this new Italian restaurant in town I've been wanting to try out."

"Wouldn't that be funny."

"What?"

"If Rex does manage to find a date for tonight, somehow I don't think his ego could handle seeing us there together. Hell, I'd pay to see his face, though."

"Knowing you, you'd ask him to join us."

"So is that a yes?"

"I guess it is," Tess answered, the tension between them slowly fading away.

"How about I pick you up at seven?"

"Seven it is." Tess rummaged through her coat pocket for a slip of paper. "Here, let me give you the address."

"I know where you live."

She couldn't contain the surprise on her face. Though

seeing as the town wasn't very big it shouldn't have been a complete shock. Still, she couldn't reply.

"I'm a cop, Tess, it's my job to know these things." Johnny turned and started for his SUV, hollering over his shoulder, "I'll see you at seven."

Tess got in her car but didn't leave. She watched, her gaze fixed on the rearview mirror, until Johnny pulled out of the parking lot.

Did that just happen?

Of course it had, but it had been unexpected. One minute she's leaving the office to spend a night alone, the next she has plans to go to dinner with Johnny. And *he* was the one who'd asked. He had come to her. Not for a shoulder to cry on, but for some simple company.

A date.

As she drove home, Tess tried to recall the last time they had been out in public together. Too many years to remember, but no one could deny that they had had some fun back then.

So much of their relationship had been based on what was going on around them at the time—family, friends and the fact that they had been kids—that she realized they had never had a chance.

Could things be different now that they were adults? Was it possible they could still have a future? Probably not... Not with all the broken emotions between them. The loss of Lindsey would be the hardest for Johnny to overcome, and Tess didn't want to be responsible for pushing him to do that this soon.

Tonight was tonight, and it was only dinner...a dinner between two friends with no expectations, friends who had once been much more. For now, she was pleased Johnny had thought enough to reach out to her, and she planned on being there for him in any way she could.

With the garage door starting to open, she impatiently waited, then eased her car through. She looked at her watch. It was going on six. She couldn't believe she'd wasted almost half an hour outside the office.

Bursting through the garage door to the kitchen, she smiled, realizing it wasn't a waste at all. Once more she reminded herself, it was only going to be dinner and nothing more.

Tess ran up the stairs, took a quick shower then dried her hair. After placing the suit she had worn that day in the bag for the dry cleaners, she went to her closet in search of an outfit for the evening.

Something simple, yet sexy...

She pulled out a pair of low-rise faded jeans and a white shirt with a deep-plunging neckline and laid them on her bed. She slid open the top drawer of her dresser, and removed the lacy thong underwear and matching white bra.

Although she prayed for a pleasant evening, she had a lot to be nervous about. She dropped her towel, misted her body with a sweet-scented spray, then proceeded to get dressed. There were still many unresolved feelings between her and Johnny Sawyer.

Even if they were from years ago.

She accessorized the outfit with a pair of diamond-studded earrings, then went to the mirror to take one last look. It seemed as though she were a kid again, going on her first date, anxiety taking over, wanting to make sure she looked perfect.

Despite her earlier thoughts, she admitted this wasn't just *any* date. Johnny had been her one true love, and she was trying desperately to restrain her expectations. Yet she couldn't deny she would give anything for the two of them to have a second chance.

She shook her head, willing the thoughts to leave her be, then headed down the stairs.

Looking out the window, she noticed how quickly the dark clouds had replaced the otherwise-blue sky. A storm was definitely brewing in the east. Just then, Tess saw Johnny's SUV going down the street away from her house.

Could it be that he was having second thoughts about taking her out? Her mind raced at the possibility.

Again, headlights caught her eye. The vehicle had turned around and was slowly driving toward her house. Trying to stay out of sight, she watched. The SUV pulled up to the curb. There wasn't any motion from within nor did any doors open.

Tess checked her makeup then grabbed her purse, ready to meet Johnny outside. An interior light lit up the vehicle. However, it wasn't Johnny sitting in front of her house, peering at her from underneath the rim of a baseball hat. The man was staring straight at Tess as if knowing exactly where she stood, wanting *her* to know he had seen her.

Who the hell...

The phone rang.

Tess practically jumped out of her skin. She looked again to the SUV. There it was, curbside, the man still looking at her, holding her gaze. The phone continued to ring. The machine picked up.

"It's me, I'm—"

Tess turned and grabbed the phone off the end table. "Johnny? Is that you?"

"Tess, are you okay?"

She turned back to the window. The vehicle, the man, he was gone.

"Tess, are you there? What the hell's going on?"

"I'm here." Her hand shook as she held the phone to her ear. "I'm fine."

"You don't sound fine."

"I had to run downstairs to get the phone, that's all," she lied. "What's up?"

"I was just calling to let you know I'm on my way, but I'm—"

The doorbell rang, and Tess screamed. Her panic couldn't be contained. "Damn it!"

"What's gotten into you?" Johnny asked. "It's me, I'm here."

The ensuing ringing of the doorbell alerted her to Johnny's presence. She walked to the door, trying to remain calm along the way, then looked through the peephole. She opened the front door, stepping back to allow him in, but he didn't make any attempt to oblige her gesture.

She hung up the phone and he did the same.

"What the hell was that scream all about?"

"Nothing, the doorbell just startled me." Tess waited, hoping he would leave it at that and come in. When he didn't, she said, "Are you ready to go?"

"Sure," he replied. He sounded a bit reluctant.

"If you've changed your mind, I'll understand." Tess prayed that wasn't the case. After seeing that strange man in front of her house, she did not want to be alone.

"Lock your door, I'm taking you out to dinner." Johnny smiled.

She went back in the house, grabbed her purse then locked up, briefly stopping on the porch, taking one last look at the empty street. Had she been seeing things? *Who the hell was that?* she worried. Was he still watching her?

"Are you sure you're all right?" Johnny's voice broke her

trance. "You seem pale."

Tess shook the thoughts from her mind, knowing if someone had been out there he couldn't get near her now. Not when she had Johnny by her side.

"I'm fine. Just hungry, I guess."

"If you say so." Johnny held her gaze for a moment, as if analyzing her, before motioning her to his vehicle.

Like the gentleman he was, he opened the passenger-side door. As Tess walked around him, the scent of his cologne spiraled up through her nostrils. It was still the same scent that had intoxicated her senses all those years ago.

Johnny had never been one for change.

They drove to the restaurant in silence with only the sound of the light drizzle from the rain hitting the windshield. Tess turned her head a little to the left to see his face. His grief was still apparent, and he looked as though he hadn't slept in days.

She was starting to think maybe this dinner wasn't such a good idea after all. What would they talk about? Did he really need the added stress of wondering which way their conversations would go?

But it had been Johnny's suggestion to go to dinner. He had reached out to *her*, and she wanted him to know he could turn to her for anything.

"What's wrong?" he asked.

"Why would you think there was something wrong?"

"You're quiet."

"I guess I'm afraid I'll say the wrong thing."

"Such as..."

"I mean, asking you how you're coping is a pretty stupid question, yet it's a simple one. I don't know... I wish the air didn't feel so thick between us."

56

"I don't want you to feel that way. Whatever you ask, I'll always give you an honest answer." Johnny braked for the red light.

"I know."

"If I'm honest with myself, I think I'm on my way to accepting Lindsey's death." Johnny exhaled. "If only I could stop feeling guilty for doing so..."

"Lindsey will never be forgotten, but you're still here, Johnny, you can't stop living."

"You're right, but it doesn't change how I feel."

"How are the Morans?" Tess asked, wanting to slightly change the subject before they both became entrapped in the tragedy all over again.

"I wouldn't know. I've had to take myself out of that whole atmosphere. I know they're devastated by the loss of their daughter, but I can't handle being reminded about it through their tears. Isn't that awful of me?"

"No." Tess glanced out her window. "People deal with grief in different ways. If it helps you to be away from them, then you have to do what's best for you."

"You always did understand me."

"I'm sure they understand, too."

"Maybe." He shrugged.

"Lindsey wouldn't want you to be tearing yourself up either."

"I'm not so sure about that." Johnny turned right on Central Boulevard, then pulled into the restaurant parking lot.

"What do you mean?"

"Forget it."

"That's the second time you've made a remark like that."

"I said forget it." Johnny turned off the SUV, then went around to open her door.

Even though she wanted to, Tess didn't pursue the subject. Now more than ever, she knew something was eating away at him, something deeper than the death of his wife. The comment a few seconds ago and the one back at the cemetery hinted at some inner secret.

What didn't he want her to know?

Inside the bistro, the aroma of homemade Italian food filled her nose. Her stomach growled, forcing her to realize how hungry she was. She followed close behind Johnny as he gave the woman behind the wooden podium his last name. Tess wouldn't have thought he had taken the time to make a reservation, or that they needed one, but right away they were led to a table for two in the back corner of the room.

Johnny pulled out Tess's chair, waiting for her to sit, then took the seat across the table. Not long after that, a waitress appeared with menus, making their drink orders first priority. Johnny ordered a draft and smiled when Tess ordered a glass of Merlot.

"What's that smirk about?"

"I don't know how you can drink that stuff." He cringed. "Lindsey used to drink the same— I'm sorry."

"Don't be." Tess smiled. "Lindsey and I were a lot alike."

"In some ways," Johnny agreed with reluctance.

"Anyway, *you* don't have to drink it." Tess opened the burgundy menu that had been placed in front of her, getting pure satisfaction out of being able to make Johnny smile again.

That smile melted her heart tonight as much as it had the first time she ever saw it.

Tess ordered veal parmesan, and Johnny settled for a big

plate of lasagna. While they waited for their meals, he asked about her job and Tess asked him the same. The conversation was standard of a blind date, to say the least, but she was comfortable with it.

So was Johnny.

When the food came, Tess couldn't help notice how much he was savoring the meal. The poor guy probably hadn't eaten a decent supper in months, and he wasn't having any trouble finishing it tonight. Tess, on the other hand, was stuffed after eating half of her dish.

"Ah, come on, you can do better than that." Johnny washed down the last of his beer.

"I can't eat another bite." She blotted the corners of her mouth with the cloth napkin, then placed it on the table. "But be my guest."

"I'm good. Do you want another glass of wine?"

"I don't know... Are you going to have another drink?" Tess asked, not wanting to draw out the meal unless that was what he wanted.

"I could go for another beer."

"Well then, this round's on me!"

There was no need for Tess to try placing the voice, for she knew who it was before Mike approached their table. This was not what she needed. Johnny and Tess had managed to get through dinner, and all Mike would do was put a damper on the rest of their evening.

He'd always been good at ruining the moment, she reminded herself.

"That's quite all right," Johnny responded, looking beyond his friend. "Who'd you drag here with you tonight?"

"Some hot little redhead I pulled over this afternoon." Mike winked at Johnny. "I think the more important question is, what're you doing here with her?"

"Hello to you, too," Tess said.

"Don't start," Johnny warned Mike. "Thanks to Tess, I'm not sitting at home alone tonight."

"Yeah, I'm sure." Mike looked down at Tess with piercing eyes.

"I asked Tess to have dinner with me—not that it's any of your business." Johnny signaled to the waitress for the check, obviously having thought twice about staying at the restaurant a second longer. "You'd better get back to your date. She just might leave with the busboy."

Tess couldn't help snicker at Johnny's remark, and if looks could kill, she would have been in grave trouble by the way Mike glared down at her in response.

"Why don't you two join us?" Mike asked, in a deliberate attempt to take control of the time Tess and Johnny were spending together.

"I think we'll pass. Unless you'd like to spend the evening with Mike and his new redhead?" Johnny asked Tess.

All she had to do was roll her eyes, and she had Johnny again giving her that gorgeous smile of his.

"Don't say I didn't offer." Mike gave them both a final look-over, knowing he'd been defeated, before going back to his table.

"He can be a real ass sometimes," Johnny said.

"Yeah, most of the time, but he doesn't bother me."

"Even so..." Johnny looked across the room at the table where Mike sat. "I don't know if I want to hang around here and wait for him to bring the redhead to us."

"Me either."

After Johnny paid the bill, leaving a generous tip on the table, the two of them headed out the door. Tess first with Johnny's hand lightly placed on the small of her back, his touch immediately bringing back all her unresolved desires.

Dinner had gone exceptionally well with much of the night still left. Tess wasn't sure what Johnny's plans were, but prayed he didn't intend to end the night just yet.

Chapter Four

The rain outside had grown stronger during the two hours they had spent having dinner. They ran to his vehicle with Johnny leading Tess to the driver's side. He unlocked the door, Tess jumped in and Johnny slid in beside her.

They'd been laughing when Johnny had dropped his keys in the attempt to quickly unlock the door, but now, as they shared the bucket seat behind the steering wheel, their gazes locked.

She could almost feel his heart beating as his gaze penetrated her skin. If it were anyone else, she would've felt uneasy being trapped in such an intense moment. But she didn't—not now—not with Johnny Sawyer.

She hadn't been this close to him since...

Since the last time they had made love. How long had that been, eleven, twelve years? A lifetime ago, yet Tess could still remember how it had felt to be taken by this man.

Her gaze fell to Johnny's mouth. In that second, there wasn't anything she wouldn't give up to have his lips touch hers again. The memories of the intimacy they had shared came flooding back as if no years had passed between them...years filled with sorrow, with regret and worst of all, death.

She knew it was dangerous to be thinking this way, to want him, yet she couldn't move.

She should have climbed into her own seat but was frozen with Johnny pushed against her. Maybe it was the ever-changing look in his eyes that held her there, crushed between him and the center console, a look of sadness—confusion perhaps—slowly fading away, becoming filled with passion.

Johnny held her attention as he touched the side of her face, the wetness from the rain cool on her cheek. His closed eyes opened, blinked again. Johnny pulled back, leaving Tess with a deep sense of emptiness.

Suddenly, she felt the release. The line of electricity that had held them there in his seat, frozen in time, had been broken. Tess climbed over to her seat.

Johnny wiped the rain from his face, then looked at Tess. The tension was gone from his eyes, along with the confusion, the desire, as though the last few minutes had never happened. A low laugh escaped his mouth, reacting to Tess's appearance as if noticing her for the very first time since climbing back into the vehicle.

"We're soaked." He ran his fingers through the sides of his dark hair.

"This wasn't what I had in mind tonight." Tess muffled a laugh, still a bit on edge, not knowing what to make of Johnny's sudden change.

"No, but a guy could find himself in worse places." Johnny looked down at Tess's drenched clothes.

The fact that she had on a white shirt had slipped her mind. By the seduction in Johnny's eyes, Tess was sure the white material wasn't holding up too well against the rain. Her first reaction was to cross her arms over her chest, but she stopped herself. His attitude, bouncing back and forth, was getting the best of her, and she wanted it to stop. Tess held her position, raising her eyebrows at him.

"I see you're enjoying yourself here," she commented, no longer caring about the white clinging material. It wasn't as though Johnny was seeing something he hadn't seen before.

"Is that what I'm doing?"

"I think you are." She teased him, pleased he was relaxed again.

So was she.

"I think you're beautiful."

Johnny's response wasn't what she expected. Tess wasn't even sure if he knew what he'd said, but his actions clarified everything. Turning slightly in the seat, he leaned in.

Tess watched his every move, speechless, as Johnny's gaze traveled to her mouth. He continued to inch forward, slowly, cautiously, and Tess felt as though she were dreaming. Then, in a flash, his mouth was close, barely touching hers.

The kiss was soft. Tess gave in to his touch as he placed a damp hand under her hair, behind her neck. The way they explored each other's mouths was from years of practice, as if they'd never been apart.

Time seemed to stand still.

There were no thoughts of Lindsey, Johnny's loss or how long it had been since they'd found themselves together like this. Only a pure desire for a love that had once been strong yet lost in the confusion of adolescence. Being in his arms again only elucidated the truth...

Johnny Sawyer had never left Tess's heart.

He pulled back—not quite an inch—resting his forehead on hers. She felt as though he was searching her eyes, searching for an answer to explain the here and now. Was it to further his pleasure, to ease his guilt or purely to reassure himself that it was okay for them to be in each other's arms?

Tess explored every inch of his face, his eyes, his faint smile, the creases at his brow from the months of stress he had endured. She feared that a kiss like that would be their last, especially if his guilt, his loss, began to overpower the reason he had brought his lips to hers to begin with. She wanted to savor every second of it.

"I'm sorry," he said, releasing her hands, pulling away again.

"For kissing me?"

"I guess." He looked out at the rain, steadier now, its wet blanket covering the windshield, then back to Tess. "I didn't set out for this to happen."

"It was only a kiss."

"Yeah...only a kiss."

The ringing of Johnny's cell phone brought uneasiness back into the moment. At first he let it ring, but the fact that he was always on call made him answer. Tess listened to his brief responses of *yes's* and *no's*, then to the inevitable, "I'll be right there". He hit the end button and threw the phone on the dashboard.

"Wasn't it only a couple of hours ago when you asked if I was done for the day?" Johnny started the engine.

"I suppose you never know when duty's going to call," Tess said, hoping her disappointment wasn't too apparent.

Looking out the window, she noticed Mike running from the restaurant, alone, up to Johnny's SUV.

"They called you, too?" Johnny asked as he rolled down the window.

"Yeah, I might as well ride with you." Mike jumped in the backseat without waiting for Johnny's permission. "We need to get a move on."

Johnny took the red light from the dash and positioned it up on the roof of the vehicle as the rain splattered on his face. Tess glanced back at Mike, then to the speedometer of the SUV. From the looks of things, she wasn't on her way home.

"Johnny, let me out. I'll get a cab."

"I'm not going to drop you off on the street, but I don't have time to take you home."

"Maybe you should listen to her. This is a police matter," Mike yelled from the backseat, the noise from the siren echoing throughout the street. "She has no business coming along."

"It's not as if she'll be the only spectator there." Johnny continued down the street with no signs of changing his mind.

Tess watched in silence as they blew through the streetlights ahead. She had no idea what was going on or what to expect when they arrived on the scene. When they finally reached their destination, the sight before them hit her hard.

Took her breath away.

She saw the heavy-duty Ford pickup truck first. It didn't seem to be damaged all that much. It wasn't until Johnny pulled up to the scene of the accident that she saw the second vehicle. The small compact car was folded together like an accordion, and the sight of the windshield was too much to take in.

She almost couldn't believe her eyes, thought they were playing tricks on her. Trying to blink away the image did no good. There lay a body, facedown, halfway through the glass, blood mixing with rain, the victim motionless.

The moment they stopped Johnny and Mike flew out of the vehicle. Tess didn't move from her seat. She watched as they joined the other officers and paramedics. To her left, a man, the driver of the truck, was pushed against a police car and handcuffed with force.

Apparently the man had hit the small car head on with his truck. From the way the vehicles were positioned, Tess assumed he must have driven through the intersection. Nine out of ten, he was probably on his way home from having one too many drinks at the local bar. It happened all too much in the east side of town.

Once again, Tess let her gaze rest on the badly damaged car, the body protruding from it.

Whether male or female, it didn't matter. The body looked lifeless and no doubt was. Eventually, she had to put her head down. She couldn't bring herself to watch as they pulled the body from the wreck. First she heard the smashing of the remaining glass from the windshield, then shouts from the rescue team, "Grab her!"

Her. It was a woman, somebody's wife, mother, somebody's heartache.

It was then that Tess thought of Lindsey and how she must have looked at the accident. Had she, too, been lunged through the windshield from the negligence of not having worn her seatbelt? Along with the thought, a cold chill of despair seared through Tess.

Johnny...

What was this doing to him? This accident would painfully bring back the tragedy of seeing Lindsey lying dead in her car. Just when Tess thought it was possible for Johnny to be coming out of his shell, the chance of that surely had gone up in smoke the minute his cell phone rang.

Tess waited, not moving an inch, until she heard the driver-side door open. She slowly turned her head to see Johnny climb in, starting the SUV in the process. He didn't speak a word, didn't make a sound, but the look on his face was haunted. Tess couldn't begin to know what to say to him.

She didn't even try.

Again they drove through the streets in silence, leaving Mike at the scene. When Johnny pulled up her driveway, she wasn't sure if she was relieved to be home or worried that he would now be alone to deal with his demons.

He clearly still struggled with many of them. She could see the pain he'd managed to hide for that evening resurface all over again. Despite not knowing what to do for him, she wanted to be there if he needed her, to be someone for him to talk to. But he didn't look like a man who wanted to talk. Be that as it may, for his sake, she needed to try.

"Why don't you come in?"

"I have to go back to the station and fill out the report on the accident." He shook his head, staring off in the distance.

"Can't one of the other police officers do that?"

"It's not the report I have a problem with." Johnny pinched the bridge of his nose, closing his eyes to the stress of the situation. "I don't think I can face that girl's family."

"Isn't Mike dealing with that?" No one had said as much, but it was unthinkable for Tess to believe that Johnny would be made to do that so soon after dealing with his own loss. "You're trying to deal with too much as it is. I don't think it would be good for you."

"It's my job."

"Is there anything I can do?" Tess asked, knowing there wasn't.

"I'm sorry you had to witness that."

Never once did he look at her. Tess waited only a minute to make sure their conversation was over, then opened the door. There was so much she wanted to say—to do—but couldn't find the words. She held on to her purse as she got out of the SUV, then faced him before shutting the door.

"Don't subject yourself to more than you have to. It'll only bring it all back."

"It's never left," he said, putting the vehicle in gear.

She knew it was too good to be true to think that Johnny could have put that part of his life aside for even one night. His statement told her as much, and it pierced her heart, causing a twinge of pain—or maybe, selfishly, it was resentment—to take over her.

What was there to be resentful of—the ghost of Lindsey and the fact that she still haunted Johnny's thoughts every minute of every day? If that was the case, Tess knew she could never compete with that. She was starting to think crazy. For God's sake, that accident tonight would have been enough to put a normal person over the emotional edge let alone Johnny who was already messed-up to begin with.

Tess closed the door and stepped back. At a slow pace she walked up the sidewalk to her front door, only glancing back when Johnny reached the street and took off, squealing wet tires down the road, all thoughts of the earlier, unexplained visitor vacant from her mind.

The rain had let up, but it still was quite chilly when she entered the house. She threw her purse across the kitchen countertop and opened the cupboard above the sink to get a glass. She was never one to drink alone, but tonight she needed to soothe away the pain.

She looked at the wooden wine rack, which, up until now, had been used as a decorative tool to suit the modern-style kitchen, then removed a bottle of blackberry Merlot. Hell, she wasn't even sure she had a corkscrew to open the old bottle. Lucky for her, the wine had been cheap, and had a removable cap.

Tess went to the gas fireplace and lit a match. If someone saw her now, they would think she was crazy to be starting a fire. It was the end of summer but still a ways away before she would have to worry about the cold weather.

Grabbing her glass of wine, Tess sat on the white fluffy rug, enabling the fire to warm the chills from her skin. It did nothing for her mind. The dampness of the tepid liquid on her lips brought back the feeling of Johnny's kiss, warm, sweet, unexpected.

She couldn't forget it.

Watching the amber flames dance along the logs calmed her. And after losing herself in her thoughts for more than an hour, Tess felt she was ready to go upstairs and crawl into bed.

But her body wouldn't move.

If only she had someone to share these lonely nights with, her life would be complete. Whether it was the wine or the warmth from the fire, Tess relaxed her head back on the oversized pillow and fell into a deep sleep, reveling in her hopes for a lost dream.

CZ

Johnny went back to the station. As expected, the entire place was in an uproar. The father of the woman involved in the crash was demanding to see the man who had killed his daughter. Of course, the police would never allow that, seeing as the man had been booked on a felony drunk-driving warrant, but there was little they could do to calm the father down.

Johnny felt for the man, felt his pain and his need for retribution, but that didn't change the way he looked at Johnny, in anger, a cop who was holding him back. Knowing his remorse wouldn't give the man any comfort, Johnny left the front cubicle of the police station and took refuge in his office.

The dreaded report was sitting on his desk, waiting for the standard answers to be typed in. He did so, as quickly as possible, the details of the accident hammering within his head, reminding him of Lindsey, her death, the lies, the unanswered questions that lingered with each passing day.

After filing the report, Johnny stepped out of his office only to find the commotion in the front of the station was still raging in full force. He took a left down the long corridor, then went out the back door, leaving the station without so much as a word to anyone. It wasn't until he was almost in his vehicle that he heard Mike approaching from behind.

"Wait up."

Johnny continued, ignoring his partner, climbing into the driver's side, slamming the door shut. He started the engine, almost succeeded in leaving, but Mike flung open the door and jumped into the seat next to him.

"I can't believe they called you on this one," Mike said. "I know it's been six months since Lindsey—"

"It's done." Johnny glared at him. "All I want to do now is get the hell out of here."

"I think you need to go home and call it a night."

"What I needed was for *you* to have filled out that damn report! It was bad enough seeing that girl stuck through the window of a car, but I would've thought you'd have saved me the hassle of going through it again on paper."

"Look man, I wasn't the one who put it on your desk. I'm sorry you had to go through that, but it's over now. There's no reason why we can't forgot this night ever happened," Mike said in his *let's chalk it up to a normal night's work* attitude.

"Yeah, until the next time something like this happens to

remind me that my wife was torn to pieces in the same kind of tragedy." Johnny started the SUV, then turned his attention to Mike. "Can I drop you off somewhere?"

"Why don't you come back to the restaurant with me?"

"You don't need me. I'm sure your bimbo's still waiting for you."

"What the hell's your problem!" Mike asked. "For someone who's still hung up on the past, you seemed to be having quite the time with Tess tonight. Or has it always been that way with you...stuck in the past?"

"Quit trying to analyze me."

"Don't you see she's only using Lindsey's death as a way to get you back?"

"I've had about enough of you!" Johnny slammed his fist on the steering wheel, glaring at Mike. "Not once, since everything's gone down, has Tess thrown herself at me. I was the one who asked her out, and you want to know something?"

"What?" Mike lit a cigarette then blew the smoke out the half-opened window.

"I wish to God I would've never gotten that call tonight. Now get the hell out of here!"

"Just like old times... You're going to let her come between our friendship, aren't you?"

"You have it all backward," Johnny shot back. "I should've never let you get between Tess and me all those years ago."

As soon as the words left his mouth, he couldn't believe he'd said them. *Is that how I really feel?* The thought had crossed his mind after their breakup years ago, but now? He pondered on it for a moment... In spite of the recent loss of his wife, he couldn't help that he truly felt that way deep inside.

"I'm sure Lindsey would be really happy to hear that," Mike

said as if reading Johnny's mind.

He got out of the SUV, slamming the door on Johnny without further word. An argument with Mike was the last thing he needed in his life right now. He knew his friend was only trying to help, but Johnny didn't need to hear it.

Didn't *want* to hear it.

Mike had been his best friend as far back as Johnny could remember, and he had learned to deal with his demeanor. Now, as an adult, Johnny wasn't going to let him impinge on his life like that any more.

As he came upon the dirt road leading to his new property, Johnny stopped the vehicle, thought twice about going home. What he really felt like doing was hitting the local bar, drinking himself into oblivion.

What would that accomplish? It would help him to forget, but as soon as the buzz wore off, he'd be right back in the hell that was now his life. The last thing he wanted to do was follow in the steps of so many other cops, too many of whom were drunks.

He kept straight on the main highway, his destination still unclear. He looked at the empty seat next to him. To have Tess there again would be good for him right now. He had enjoyed her company. It had been comforting to be free of all the pain and guilt for a little while, anyway, to be with the one person who knew him the best.

He thought, in due time, he'd be able to get through the grief and confusion all on his own. Even so, he desperately wanted to let Tess in. To tell her everything, the whole story of his life with Lindsey, to tell her how sorry he was for letting her down in the past. But he didn't think he had the strength or the courage to do so.

It would only portray him as a coward. He should've

worked things out with Tess back then, but she'd wanted so much more than he'd been willing to give, being as they were both barely out of high school, inexperienced kids.

Months after the relationship ended, Johnny had tried reaching out to Tess, but she'd been too hurt to respond to his attempts. In the end, he had settled for her best friend. He hated himself for thinking about his dead wife as a second choice, but the realization erupted into the truth.

How long have I felt this way? Johnny was too tired to sort through the years. The past was the past and all he had was the future. With that came more questions, and the detective in him needed to find answers.

Or was it forgiveness?

When he reached Tess's, he didn't pull up the driveway. He parked in the street and shut off the engine, unclear as to what he expected to find there. It was closing in on midnight, and the house was dark except for a tawny glow illuminating her living room. It wasn't a normal light, the way it flickered... He stiffened. *Fire.*

He blasted out of his SUV, running up to the house, to her window, in a panic...

Immediately, the stupidity of his fear hit him dead over the head. The fireplace was lit, blazing away in the darkness. What had he been thinking? Had he really thought her house was on fire? His panic proved his point that he was dangerously on edge these days.

He couldn't stand it.

He didn't want to assess his life day by day with thoughts that the worst was going to happen. Ever since seeing Lindsey, dead in her car, he'd known the instant reactions of dread would be set in his mind forever—only stronger now than before.

He stood, looking through the window, not knowing where to turn, wondering why he was allowing himself to care for someone this soon, to be her savior. Tess didn't need saving, so why was he reaching out to ring her doorbell?

Johnny brought his hand to his side, took a step back, wanting to get as far away from her house, this town, his life as he could, knocking over a large clay pot of flowers in the process. If the pot had been plastic, it wouldn't have made near the noise that the ceramic one did as it crashed to pieces all around him.

"Son of a..." he whispered.

There was no sneaking away now. The previously darkened room was suddenly lit in a strong blaze. Tess had heard the commotion, too. Johnny waited for the front door to fly open, for Tess to witness his embarrassment, but nothing happened.

He went back to the window, saw Tess, fumbling with the phone, shaking, without doubt calling 911. This time Johnny managed to ring the bell and knock on the door, calling out her name as he did so.

"Tess, it's Johnny, open up." He leaned back over to the window.

Their gazes locked. He watched her lips as she talked into the phone before hanging up. He had scared the hell out of her. Johnny waited until the door finally opened. A sleepy, petrified Tess stood in the doorway.

"Johnny." Tess gasped, looking down at the broken pieces of the pot. "What're you doing?"

"Would you believe that I tripped?" He went to her, held her by the shoulders, trying to stop the quivering. "I'm sorry I scared you."

She exhaled. "I never knew a cop could be so obvious." She looked toward the darkened street, for what, he didn't know, trying to regain her composure. "Aren't you guys trained to be sneaky?"

"You'd think so, wouldn't you?" He smiled. "Again, I'm sorry."

"Did you see anyone else out here?"

Nervousness lingered about her.

"No. Why?" He bent down, picking up the larger pieces of the pot. "Has something happened?"

"You surprised me, that's all." Tess leaned against the door casing, nodding at the mess. "Just leave it. I'll clean it in the morning."

"Maybe this wasn't such a good idea." Johnny felt foolish.

"And what would that be? You peeping through my windows in the middle of the night?"

"That too." He put his hands in the pockets of his jeans, wondering if he should run for the SUV or take her in his arms and hold her close. At least she seemed to be calm, now that she knew there wasn't a stranger at her door.

"Do you want to come in?"

"Looks like I woke you up."

"Why would you think that?" Tess asked, patting down her hair.

He smiled at her reaction, then nodded inside.

"I guess I must've fallen asleep by the fire."

"About that... Why do you have a fire lit this time of year?"

"Trying to burn the chill out of my body." Tess rubbed at her arms.

"Yeah, I know what you mean."

"Why don't you come in, and I'll make some coffee." Tess started to head back in the house but turned around. "Unless you have plans to peer into someone else's window tonight."

"You're a smartass."

"You always liked that about me."

"Yes, I did."

Johnny followed Tess into the house, closing the door behind him. Earlier when he had picked her up, he hadn't taken the time to look around the place. After Tess disappeared into the kitchen, he did just that.

She'd done real well for herself. The house was attractive and situated in one of the newer sections of town. If he remembered correctly, the cul-de-sac had been built a few years ago. The walls were decorated with pictures, with flower swags above each and every one of them.

Tess had always had a real knack for that sort of thing. Even though neither of them had had a whole lot of money back then, she had managed to put her mark on the apartment they had shared. And when she'd left—what seemed a lifetime ago— that part of her had always stayed with him.

When Tess returned from the kitchen, Johnny was still standing on the earth-toned tile of the front foyer. He felt anything but comfortable in her house.

"Do you want to talk about it?"

"Not really." Johnny continued admiring the spacious room, avoiding eye contact. "I'm sorry you had to see that tonight. The accident."

"Not as sorry as I am that you had to go through it." Tess moved in, until she was standing mere inches from him. "That had to be so horrible for you."

"You don't know the half of it."

"All right, that's it." Tess threw her arms in the air. "That's the second time tonight you've made a remark like that. What's going on with you?"

"Oh, I don't know." He raised his voice. "In the last year I failed to protect my wife and lost my sanity in the process. Tonight I had to witness another woman die before her time. I don't know, Tess, do you think I'm being a little melodramatic?"

He hadn't meant to take that tone with her, but these days, he couldn't help it. He snapped at everything, everybody, his partner, Ted Jennings, now Tess. Every hour, every minute, every second, he felt as though his mind was going to blow into a million pieces.

"I never said you were being melodramatic, but I've heard you make these comments *before* you ever went to that accident scene tonight."

"I don't know what you're talking about."

But he did. He knew exactly what statements she had picked up on.

"Back at the cemetery and right before we went into the restaurant, and I don't appreciate you insinuating that I'm accusing you of anything." Fury filled her. "I didn't ask you to come back here tonight, you know. As a matter of fact, I haven't asked anything of you!"

"No, you haven't." Johnny turned to go for the door.

"Damn it, Johnny, how long are you going to keep this all bottled up inside?"

Her voice stirred something deep within him. No matter how badly he wanted to storm out that door, he couldn't. The feeling inside only grew, taking over his entire being. He went and stood directly in front of her, staring down into her shocked eyes.

Whatever was going through his body couldn't be contained. He didn't want to further the conversation, yet he didn't want to walk out on her either. He wanted all the pain to go away, to vanish into thin air as if it had never happened. He wanted to be a kid again, the same kid who had been madly in love with Tess Fenmore. For just a moment, he wanted to be free of all the horrific feelings ripping him apart.

More than anything, he wanted Tess.

Before he lost his nerve, he pulled Tess into his arms, covering her mouth with his. The room started to spin as if they were in another dimension...a different place...a different time, and he realized there was nothing stopping him...nothing to hold them in the present.

He wanted to go back, take Tess back to a time when all that mattered was the two of them. Right at that moment they were free to let go of all that was going on around them...free to let their bodies take over, to reconnect, to feel what it had been like when they'd been young and in love.

Tess seemed stunned when Johnny made his move. His lips trailed from her mouth to her neck, then back again. But she didn't refuse his touch, and her body pressed closer to his with every caress of his tongue.

If he had been with any other woman, Johnny would have chalked it up to an easy way to forget his problems, to a night full of meaningless, no-strings-attached sex. But this wasn't just any woman he was about to carry up the staircase and make passionate love to.

No...

Tess was a girl he had once loved as much as any teenage boy could. And throughout the years, every time he had laid eyes on Tess, even while married to Lindsey, he had still felt something awaken from deep within him.

Suddenly Tess backed away slightly, far enough so he could look into her eyes. The expression on her face was complex. Confusion, wanting and fear seemed to be all wrapped up in one multifaceted look. She seemed to be after something, answers maybe, verification that he was ready for this, that she was ready?

But he didn't want to talk, not now. All he wanted to do was live in the moment and never let her go. More importantly, he wanted her to indulge in the same sinful pleasures.

However, he would never force himself on Tess—or any other woman for that matter. He was sure of the things that were probably running through her mind, especially with the impulsiveness of his actions, the past and the stress of the here and now. If there was something she needed to say, he would listen.

He started to move back, a little bit farther, but it felt too good to be close to her again. He knew Tess could feel his desire stirring as he pushed against her.

He didn't move all that much.

He rubbed the edge of his thumb lightly along her lower lip, then brushed aside her bangs from her beautiful eyes. He took a deep breath, preparing himself for the shutdown to a night that had turned into a fantasy. Her warm breath grazed his hand as the words left her lips.

"You don't know how long I've waited for this." Tess leaned up, gently trailing his neck with light kisses.

Her words couldn't have pleased him more.

"I can tell you..." Johnny paused, never wanting to speak the truth as much as he did right then. "I've wanted it more than you could ever imagine."

Johnny again took the sweet taste of her mouth in his, but something made him stop. The guilt. A faint voice inside his head demanded him to stop. Warned him not to cross the line. As quickly as the voice penetrated his head, it faded in the distance, his trembling body begging his mind to throw away all restraint.

Tess must have noticed the change in him, for she held his gaze with an even stare. As she searched his face, Johnny felt the last of the guilt slowly slip away. All he could think about was holding her closer, taking her breath away with the urgency of his kiss, making love to Tess Fenmore as if it were his dying wish.

"Johnny..." Tess lightly caressed his face. "We don't have to do this."

She started to pull back, but he couldn't let her walk away. Not now. He would be full of regret. Johnny couldn't let this moment pass him by. He drew her back in, holding her firmly against the length of his body, wanting to make her feel like she'd never felt before, wanting to tell her how much he...

"I want you." He leaned in close as he held the back of her neck securely in his hand, positioning her right where he wanted her.

"If that's what you truly want—"

"I do."

"Then please...don't stop."

Johnny felt the weight lifting off his shoulders. All the guilt, the pain and the confusion, it was all gone, rising up through the air like a puff of smoke. It was as if the last few months, years, of his life had never taken place. It was though he were nineteen again, nineteen and still in love with the woman of his dreams.

Chapter Five

Tess felt as if she had died and gone to heaven. What she felt for Johnny at the moment had nothing to do with all the nights she had spent alone, wishing things could have been different between them. Nor was it about the regrets she had for what had happened all those years ago. What she felt right now, nestled in Johnny's arms, was a pure desire to be loved by him in every way possible.

With no looking back.

His touch was different than she remembered. They weren't kids any more and experience had grown with the years that had passed between them. She was feeling it now in the way he touched her, the way he took the time to make her feel as though she was the only woman who mattered. His breath, his kiss, his hands trailing along her smooth, burning skin... If the world were to end tomorrow, she would die a happy woman.

Though they couldn't have been more than twelve feet from the fireplace, Johnny picked her up and carried her to the white fur rug she had fallen asleep on a few hours before.

She found it hard to breathe, the same way she'd felt when Johnny had kissed her earlier that night, as though being suffocated by an unknown force, an inner passion that had been dormant for years, waiting for this moment to give it life again. At the same time, Johnny provided her with all the oxygen she needed.

His mouth rarely left hers, only to trace her neck and shoulders with his kisses. Stirring beneath him, savoring his touch, Tess suddenly found herself afraid. Afraid this would be the last time she would feel his body against hers. But she couldn't let her worries take her out of the moment. Not now, not after dreaming about this for years.

All she wanted was Johnny Sawyer and everything he could give her.

Obviously putting his own needs aside, Johnny didn't rush. He lay there, kissing her, for what felt like an eternity before taking the time to remove her clothes, his lips only leaving her body long enough to pull the white shirt over her head and undo the discreet front clasp of her lacy bra.

From that instant on, Tess allowed herself to give in to everything happening between them, no worries holding her back. She was lost in time. She didn't realize when exactly they became fully unclothed. The warmth of the fire was no longer necessary, for the heat from Johnny's body was all she needed...

She felt eleven years younger, at a time when they had still shared a life together. Though the sex had always been wonderful between them, never could she recall the intimacy being this close. The way his touch now seared her skin... It was breathtaking.

Gazing into his eyes, she could tell he was as captivated by her as she was by him. How long would it last? What would this do to Johnny? Would he look at her and be filled with regret after their lovemaking was over?

Johnny had been with Lindsey for many years, and now

she was gone. Tess had seen what Lindsey's death had done to him, even if she hadn't quite understood the hidden guilt he carried on his shoulders.

She knew it wasn't realistic to expect more out of this. However, that was exactly what she wanted. It had taken so long to put each and every one of the feelings she had for him to rest all those years ago, and now—in a split second—they were back, stronger than ever.

So was the hurt.

As the reality entered her mind, she realized Johnny was looking down into her eyes. There was so much she wanted to say but couldn't. So much she wanted to ask but couldn't find the words.

"Are you okay?" Johnny lightly kissed her lips.

"Why would you ask?"

"You just seem…"

"Lost?"

"Maybe," he agreed.

"I am." Tess pushed back a loose strand of his hair, then pulled Johnny closer. "I feel lost in your arms."

"That's a good thing."

Tess couldn't say any more. All she could do was emulate his sexy smile. He again took her mouth in a ravenous kiss, and she indulged in the thrill of the moment, allowing the pleasure to fill her entire being.

She anticipated what was to come next. He traced a finger along her cheek, staring through eyes filled with seduction, down past the hollow of her neck, to her chest. She could feel the heat escaping his body as if it were pent up in the tip of that one finger.

She arched her back as Johnny teased her breast, taunting

her nipple with every brush of his thumb. Her body screamed for his mouth to take the place of his tempting hands, but Johnny still appeared to hold back, not wanting to rush.

As his hand descended the length of her body, Tess's eyes slowly closed to his touch. Never would she have imagined he could feel so good, his hand circling along her skin, forcing her to look at him as she shuddered deep inside.

His eyes were on her.

He had to know what this was doing to her. Tess broke the stare, receding out of the internal bliss, embarrassed that Johnny had witnessed her in such a vulnerable state. But it was too late. He knew he had a hold on her. His smile told as much, held something more than desire. Something that only a man could feel when touching a woman...

Pure satisfaction.

Satisfied that he was turning her into a pile of nerves, her pleasure threatening—at any second—to explode beneath his skilled touch. Tess couldn't hide the fact that she wanted him more than she'd ever wanted anything in her whole life.

And he knew it.

As his finger circled the tender skin below her belly button, Tess tried to prop herself up on one elbow. He wouldn't let her. He leaned down, gently parting her lips with his tongue to explore her mouth once more.

As the kiss progressed, Tess could feel the light caress of his fingers grazing the warm softness below. She wanted—no, needed—Johnny to touch her there, to fulfill the desire building up within. Tess didn't know how much longer she could take it without screaming out his name.

Then it happened.

As if Johnny could read her mind, or more to the point feel

the volcanic energy stirring within, he touched her...so deep that she couldn't hold back. She could feel her own muscles shattering around him, and she wanted that for him, too. To feel the pleasures only she could give him. His lips muffled the groans escaping her mouth.

She wanted Johnny now more than ever. Johnny wanted her, too.

Not even the ringing of his cell phone could pull him away from what they were about to embark on. He broke the kiss, giving his jacket a sideward glance, ignoring it.

She didn't want him to stop, yet needed to warn him of the possible urgency of the call. After all, even though it was practically the middle of the night, he was still on duty. Hadn't he told her he was *always* on duty? If the call meant there was an emergency, she didn't want to be the reason he was ignoring his job.

"Johnny," Tess whispered through his burning kiss.

He didn't stop, and she found herself once more moving uncontrollably beneath his touch. The phone stopped ringing, and Tess gave a silent thank you to whoever had been on the other end of the line. However, it didn't make a difference. The ringing again broke through her otherwise-enraptured thoughts, and she couldn't ignore it.

"Don't you think you should answer that?"

"That's the last thing I want to do," Johnny said as his mouth trailed over one breast.

"I know, but who would be calling you at this hour? It has to be important."

Johnny sat up and reached for his coat. Tess watched as he took out the cell phone and glared down at its screen. He shook his head and threw the phone on top of the coat, returning his gaze to Tess.

"Well?"

"As always, Mike has perfect timing."

"He wouldn't call this late if it wasn't about work, would he?"

"I don't plan on finding out." Johnny eased his body alongside hers, as if he'd never left, his hands all over her again. "But thanks for being so concerned."

"I just figured—"

"Now, where were we...?" Johnny's finger traced her temple, her cheekbone, then down her neck until he reached an erect nipple. "Do you really want me to call him back?"

"Don't you dare." Tess smiled as she pulled Johnny down on her.

Some people never experienced sex as tantalizing as their foreplay, but Tess wanted Johnny to take her completely, wanted to feel him inside her, feel the way Johnny used to make love to her for hours when they were teenagers. She wanted to stay trapped in this picture, to live out a dream that she thought had died a long time ago, one she had held on to for so many years.

She looked up into his smoldering eyes. "I want you."

"You don't know how bad I want you."

"Show me."

She wrapped her arms around his neck, pulling him close. Her pearl-coated fingernails stalked down his spine until they reached his lower back, begging him, gently digging into his skin, until Johnny finally met her passion.

The sound escaping him pleased her beyond belief. The way he moved only pleased her more. After all the fantasizing that had led to the forgotten dreams, Johnny was back making love to her in a way so unlike before.

CᴁƷ

Their bodies wound down along with the flames as Johnny held Tess securely in his arms. She could hear the beating of his heart against her ear, her head resting on his chest. She didn't want to speak, for fear of what was to come. For fear that he would get up and walk out on her, leaving her alone in the quiet house, to once again face the one thing missing in her life.

However, he showed no signs of leaving. He seemed to be content holding her, stroking her long brown hair with the tips of gentle fingers. It was the simplicity of his touch that made her quiver with the reality of what had happened. Had it been loneliness that brought him back to her? She wasn't sure.

She needed to know.

Tess leaned up on one arm in order to see his face. His immediate, loving smile gave her hope that his needs had been the same as hers, the urgent need to be back in each other's arms again. She didn't think she could accept any other explanation.

"Are you regretting stopping me from leaving earlier?" Johnny asked, his hands traveling down the length of her naked body.

"Should I have let you walk out?"

"What kind of answer is that?"

"What do you think?"

She wanted to tell him how she really felt, but decided it would be to her advantage to leave the ball in his court. The last thing she wanted to do was pressure him with all the undying words of her love that threatened to slip past her lips. It was way too soon to be giving in to the crazy fantasy that they could just pick up where they had left off eleven years ago.

"I don't know how you feel, but I'm glad you stopped me from walking out that door." He nodded to the front of the house.

Tess repositioned her head against his chest, wrapping one arm around him, thinking about what he had said. He seemed glad he had stayed, but what exactly did that mean? Could it be possible they could have something more than one night, this soon after Lindsey's death?

Disrupting her thoughts, Johnny lifted them both so he was sitting up, his back resting on the oversized pillows with Tess lying against him.

"What's wrong?" he asked, tilting her chin with his index finger, giving Tess no choice but to look him in the eyes.

"It's strange..." Tess paused, wanting her words to come out right, wanting them to portray her true feelings.

"What's that?"

"I never thought we could be like this again."

"You've thought about us?"

"Too much."

"Me, too." Johnny bent down, lightly grazing her lips with the wake of his kiss.

"I find that hard to believe." Suddenly her mood turned from professing her feelings to wanting to know how Johnny could've had room for two women in his heart, the betrayal of the past coming back in force. "I mean... After we ended things, it wasn't long before you married. I guess I always assumed you must've found something in Lindsey that I couldn't give you. You two were together for so many years, in love, I can't imagine you looking back on us, what we had."

She closed her eyes. A lone tear escaped.

"I've regretted what took place between us since the

moment it happened, and I've never forgiven myself for the look in your eyes that day."

"The day you ended things or the day I found you in bed with my best friend?"

Suddenly the years didn't seem distant any more.

"Tess…"

"I'm sorry. I shouldn't have said that."

"Don't be. It was a rotten thing for me to do. But don't think for one second that I ever cheated on you or had feelings for Lindsey when you and I were together." Johnny pulled her close. "I let so many outside forces get in our way, Mike, your mother…" He looked down at her. "If we're going to be honest, you have to admit, we were just kids back then. I guess I wasn't ready to grow up just yet."

"I understood that."

Johnny raised his eyebrows.

"Not when you ended it, of course, but I did, in time. That's why I went to your apartment that day, to tell you I understood."

"Why didn't you answer my calls, then? Why did you make Lindsey be the go-between? You know I wanted you back. You told Lindsey there wasn't anything I could do to fix things, that I'd hurt you too badly. You told her it was over—that you didn't want anything to do with me.

Tess jerked back. "What? *What?* Lindsey said that?"

Lindsey had told him that she didn't want to see him. And Johnny—he'd just taken her word for it. Okay, they'd only been teenagers, but how could Lindsey have betrayed her like that? And why hadn't Johnny fought harder to get her back?

"And you just took her word for it, didn't bother to make the extra effort to tell me yourself?" Tess was humiliated that

Lindsey had twisted the situation to her benefit.

"Are you saying that—?"

"I had no idea. She played us both for fools, and you made it damn easy for her to do it."

Tess stood, letting the conversation get the best of her, feeling eighteen all over again. She disappeared into the bathroom, leaving Johnny to stew in the deception, oblivious to the current pain in his life, wanting him to feel the pain of her past.

⚃

After Tess heard the front door shut she emerged from the bathroom, waiting for Johnny's headlights to disappear down the driveway before entering the living room. Part of her was ashamed for acting like a child, hiding out in the bathroom instead of finishing their conversation, sorting through the misunderstandings, the lies that had torn them apart. But the other part of her, the one that filled her now, was angry, hurt and confused as hell for allowing herself to get sucked back into a part of her life she'd just as soon forget.

And he had left.

Once again, Johnny Sawyer hadn't waited around to work things out. No, he'd taken the easy road. She hadn't planned on staying holed up in the bathroom forever, just long enough to make sense of everything he had told her. None of it mattered now.

He was gone.

Tess went to the fireplace, picking up the glass of unfinished wine from hours before. She sat on the white rug, rested her body back against the pillow. Something caught her eye. She reached down and pulled the black button-up shirt from under the pillow. Johnny had worn it over a T-shirt. She held it close, the scent of his cologne washing over her. She closed her eyes, inhaling deep—it was as if he were still there, holding her in his arms.

If only...

There were too many *if only's*.

Tess didn't know how to feel, didn't know what to make out of the events of the past. She was filled with desire, with pleasure, with thankfulness for having been in Johnny's arms again. But nothing had changed. Till this day, the betrayal had clouded their happiness, even if it had only lasted a few hours. What scared her most was she knew what it felt like to have him taken up and out of her life.

Would that be the case again?

Tess sighed. Why had she handled things that way? Here she was, talking down on Johnny for leaving her, walking away from the problem at hand. Yet she'd done the very same thing by stomping to the bathroom, pouting like a bratty little child.

She looked at the crystal clock on the mantle of the fireplace. It was too late to make things right with him now. Pulling her tired body up off the floor, wanting nothing more than to go upstairs and sleep all the bad memories away, Tess was taken aback by the ringing of the phone. Again she looked at the clock.

Could Johnny be calling? Who else would it be at this hour? Had he been thinking of her, too, hopefully calling with the same regrets Tess had been dwelling on?

She picked up. "Before you say anything, I want you to know I'm sorry. I shouldn't have blamed you." She waited for him to say something, but there was no response. "Hello? Johnny, are you there?"

Still, no answer.

However, someone was definitely on the other line. Tess could hear the faint, but distinctive, heavy breathing coming from the caller. Even though the sound was barely audible, it was no less disturbing. Whoever was calling wanted Tess to know they were there.

"Hello?"

Nothing.

Suddenly, a chill took over her, as she remembered the earlier encounter with the man in front of her house, staring at her from beyond the window before Johnny picked her up for dinner.

Tess pressed the mute button on the phone, hoping whoever was doing this would think she had hung up. After a couple of seconds, she heard the click on the other end of the line. It had worked. She trembled, hoping the call had been a wrong number.

The phone rang again. Tess stared at the end table, letting it ring. When it didn't stop, she picked up.

"Hello?"

"You'll be sorry."

With her hand shaking, Tess slammed the phone down and sank deep into the cushions of the couch, looking around the room with shock and confusion exploding within her. The voice—a woman's voice—she recognized that voice.

"It's impossible," Tess found herself saying out loud.

Though she knew that there was no way it could be possible, it still didn't change the fact that she had just heard the hostile voice of a dead woman.

Chapter Six

It was well into the night when Johnny awoke from the recurring dream. Tonight, the way it ended, was different from the previous times. It was of the accident. In this dream, Johnny didn't see the lifeless body of his dead wife, but rather a peaceful Lindsey, her eyes staring deep into Johnny's soul.

Unlike the others before, when she would tell him how much she had loved him, this time she glared with hatred and said, *"Your heart has always betrayed me."*

That's when he woke up, looking at the empty space beside him. He didn't know which ate at him more—the fact that his wife wasn't there, or that he wasn't back at Tess's, holding her close, making love to her again. He knew it was his guilt that had pulled his mind into the subconscious, haunting illusions of the nightmare.

He climbed out of bed, went to the adjoining bathroom and splashed water on his face. He looked in the mirror and a stranger stared back at him, a man who felt as though he no longer had control of his life, his emotions.

He saw the last year of his life flash before his eyes, the accident, the funeral, the casket being lowered into the ground, the pregnancy test, the move, not being able to help himself from reaching out to Tess, her responding, the lies, Tess walking away from him...

They all went hand in hand, never once preventing the guilt from taking over him, forcing him to remember how many people he had hurt through it all.

But tonight something had changed, feelings in his mind had shifted, making him believe there might be a light at the end of that tunnel of hell. Tess had managed to make him forget...forget all the pain, the mystery and the guilt surrounding the awful accident.

Thinking back on the evening they had shared, after many years of being apart, made Johnny want to rush back to her, to slowly bring her out of her own dreams and into his arms.

Yet he couldn't.

He couldn't face the fact that he had hurt her, once again, having been foolish enough to believe Lindsey all those years ago. He recalled the look on Tess's face as they had made love. She had seemed peaceful lying there beneath him, her smile melting away, replaced with passion when his lips met hers.

How could he have let her go back then?

He had loved Tess so much. He still did. If only he'd been man enough to admit his mistakes, to make Tess realize the ignorance of being young was to blame for tempting him away, instead of moving on with someone else. Her best friend.

If he had taken the time back then, his life wouldn't be in shambles today. He was sure of that.

There was only one thing he could do to prevent any further heartache... He needed to forget about Tess, about his dead wife, and salvage his own life. Going on like this was bound to drive him deeper into depression, and if that were to happen, he didn't think he'd ever be able to escape it.

The sound of his cell phone shrilled through the air, bringing him out of the realm of the past. He grabbed a towel, then found his jacket, fumbling through the pockets, wanting nothing more than to cease the continuous ringing of the phone.

It was the station.

"Yeah?" he answered, pulling on his pants.

"Detective, a woman's been reported missing. The Chief wants you on the case," said the on-duty rookie officer. "He's calling for immediate action."

Johnny picked up his watch from the nightstand. It was three forty-five in the morning.

"Is there any chance that she took off?"

"The husband has sworn up and down that his wife has never been late getting home. Apparently, she was out with friends but assured him she'd be back by eleven p.m.," Officer Reinhold relayed to Johnny.

"Yeah, that's what they all say."

"What do you want me to do?"

"How old is she?" Johnny asked.

"Twenty-five."

Although they were supposed to wait twenty-four hours before investigating a missing person, it was a slow night and it wouldn't hurt for the on-duty officers to keep an eye out.

"Send out a thorough description of the woman to all the patrol cars. Tell them to scan the streets and check the alleys." Johnny gathered his clothes off a nearby chair, held them out, then threw them to the floor. "I'll be there soon."

He tossed the phone on the bed, then went to the closet, pulling out a pair of jeans, looking for his black button-up shirt. "Damn it." He had worn the shirt that night. He looked down at the pile of clothes. "Damn it." He'd left the shirt at Tess's.

The phone rang again.

"Hello?"

"Did the Chief call you?" It was his partner.

"The station did." He quickly pulled a shirt over his ruffled hair, then secured the shoulder holster, along with his gun, in place.

"The Chief's been trying to get you all night. Where the hell have you been?"

The blinking red light on his answering machine caught his eye.

"I've been asleep," Johnny lied. "Why didn't he try my cell?"

"Would that have mattered being that you've been home, asleep, having not heard your regular phone?" Mike sighed. "What the hell, Johnny, you and I both know you were at Tess's."

The last thing he wanted to do was get into a conversation with Mike about Tess. "Are you heading to the station? We've been assigned to the missing person's case."

"Your avoidance tells me I was right. You went back to her house, didn't you?"

"This small talk's going to have to wait. Are you coming in tonight, or not?" Johnny snapped.

"Unlike you, I'm already on it. Now get down here before the Chief has both our asses."

Johnny hung up the phone and was out of the house in no time flat. Work had occupied his mind lately, but Johnny was a damn good detective.

However, his resurfacing feelings for Tess had caught him off guard, filling the space in his heart that had been empty ever since the day she had walked out of his life, causing him to neglect his duties. He couldn't believe he hadn't checked his machine after getting home. He'd been out of it, pissed more than anything.

Johnny took out his cell phone. No voice mails. Why hadn't the Chief called his cell? But it wasn't a message from his boss he was hoping to find, rather one from Tess. His machine... Had she left a message on his machine?

"Focus!" Johnny demanded of his mind as he fumbled to stick the key in the ignition.

He started the SUV, attaching the red light to the roof of the vehicle for the second time that night, then tore down the road, making his job as chief detective his number-one priority.

When Johnny reached the station, the place was in chaos. In attendance were on- and off-duty officers who were trying to bring order amongst the people clogging up the entryway. He had been a cop long enough to know by the look on their faces and the tension in their voices, they were the family of the missing woman. And the man leading the pack was sure to be her husband.

Johnny prepared to face the family. It was going to be a challenge explaining to the husband that Johnny needed to play this by the book, that he couldn't officially consider his wife missing until twenty-four hours had passed since he'd last seen her.

"Detective Sawyer, am I glad to see you," Officer Reinhold said from behind the front counter. "The Chief's on line two, and he's not very happy." Reinhold nodded toward the man. "These people are going out of their minds, and they're out for our skin."

"Did you take their statements?"

"It's all in here." Reinhold opened the filing cabinet to the right of his desk and handed Johnny the folder, which had yet to be labeled. "You'd better talk to the Chief first."

Johnny let out a pent-up breath, knowing the conversation

would be anything but pleasant. He had never been one of Chief Wright's favorite people. They tended to knock heads when involved in cases of this nature, both being set in their ways on how things should be handled.

Johnny might not have the best attitude when handling people, suspects involved in these cases, but there was one thing Wright couldn't take away from him. Johnny had a real knack for breaking criminals under pressure by means of his ill-mannered tactics, and had solved many cases using it.

"Detective Sawyer."

"It's about damn time you showed up!" Chief Wright's voice wailed through the receiver.

Yep, he was pissed all right.

"I got here as quick as I could." Johnny tucked the folder under his arm.

"You better get it together, Sawyer. This isn't just any case."

"I can see that." Johnny held up a hand to the officer on his left, letting him know he'd get to the family as soon as possible. He turned his back on the chaos, lowering his voice and said, "I have to ask... Without sounding insensitive, we usually wait twenty-four hours before declaring someone missing. There could be a million reasons why this woman didn't go back home to her husband."

"Normally, I'd agree with you. But given that in the last year, we've had three women go missing—in this county alone—I think it's best that we don't wait on this one."

"I'm on it."

Johnny hung up the phone as the woman's husband barreled around the desk.

"Are you the one in charge of my wife's case?" Mark Harris

asked, clearly distraught with worry. "I want to know why you people aren't doing something to find my wife!"

"Calm down, Mr. Harris."

"I'm not going to sit here and let you brush this under the—"

Johnny stared at the man, taking in his every emotion. Johnny didn't want to tell him that the first person cops looked at when investigating a missing person's case was the husband.

"I realize you're upset, but we're not going to get anywhere if we don't have your corporation. Once I get that, we'll do our best to locate your wife." Johnny held up the folder. "I'm assuming you've already talked with one of my officers."

"Yes, I answered all their questions, told them everything I know. You people are wasting valuable time here!"

"How 'bout you let me be the judge of that." Johnny did not like being told how to do his job. "I have a few more questions for you." The man didn't fight him. "What about these friends your wife was supposedly out with?"

"What the hell's that suppose to mean—supposedly?"

"Have you contacted them?" Johnny pushed on.

"Yes, but..."

"They haven't seen her tonight, have they, Mr. Harris?" Johnny was trying to be as considerate as possible, having been through this type of scenario a million times before.

"No." Mr. Harris dropped his head, seemingly out of hurt rather than embarrassment.

"I have to ask." Johnny waited for him to look up. "Has your wife given you any inclination that she's been seeing someone else?"

"None."

"Has she ever had occasion to not come home in the past?"

"If she had, do you think I'd be here now?"

"Okay." Johnny looked down at the report. "I'm going to wait till morning, then interview your wife's friends, the ones she told you she was going out with."

"That's it? That's all you're going to do? Aren't you the same cop who lost his wife a couple of months back? How can you expect me to—"

"I know this is going to be hard, but the best thing you can do for your wife is go home. If I have any more questions for—"

"How in the hell can I go home? I need answers!"

"And we're going to get them for you. We have every available cop out there looking for her, but I need to go through this folder and get all the facts. I'll keep you posted every step of the way. You're better served at home in case she calls."

"All right, I'll do as you ask. But if you hear anything..."

"You'll be the first to know." Johnny felt for the man, knew what it was like to lose a loved one. Mark Harris reluctantly walked to the door. "Mr. Harris."

He turned to face Johnny.

"It goes both ways. If you hear from your wife, or anyone who has information about her disappearance, I want you to call us right away."

The man nodded, then, as instructed, left the station.

As Johnny turned to go to his office, a hand touched his arm and a meek voice stopped him from leaving.

"Detective."

"Can I help you?"

"My name's Janice Fellows. I'm Emily Harris's sister."

"Ms. Fellows, I can sympathize with what you're going through, but as I told your brother-in-law, it's best that you go home for now. We'll be in touch the minute we have anything to report."

"You don't understand." Johnny watched as she nervously looked toward the exit door. "There's something you should know."

By the quietness of her voice, the uneasiness of her stance, Johnny was sure this woman was about to expose something that Emily Harris's husband was unaware of. Or could it be that she had something to divulge about him? The wheels of Johnny's inquisitive mind were turning in overdrive.

"Would you be more comfortable in my office?"

"Please," she replied. Once more her gaze moved toward the front door.

Johnny led her down the short corridor, briefly stopping halfway to glance back at the sister of the missing woman, one of the many tactics he used to read people under pressure.

In his office, Johnny rounded the desk and nodded to the chair in front of it. She took a seat. He did the same, never once taking his eyes off the woman, watching as she fidgeted with the tissue in her hand.

"Why don't we get to the reason you're here, Ms. Fellows."

She nodded.

Johnny removed a pen from the Dawson Valley Police Force coffee mug, then tapped it on the yellow legal pad.

"Is it safe for me to assume that you haven't mentioned this to the other officers during their questioning?"

"I couldn't. Not with Mark there."

"He's not here now. Tell me, what is it you know?"

"My sister has been having an affair for some time now. I'm the only one who knows about it."

"And how did you come to know of this affair?"

"Emily used to have him pick her up at my house."

"Does this 'him' have a name?" Johnny leaned back in the chair, taking the notebook with him, pretending to jot down her info, but in reality, she hadn't given him anything substantial to record yet.

"She never told me his name."

"What did he look like?"

"I never saw him."

"You're not giving me much to go on here." He scratched the pen on his temple. "Is there a reason you believe that this man has done something to your sister?"

"I don't know what to think. The last time I talked to Emily—"

"Which was?"

"About three days ago."

"Go on."

"She told me she was going to break it off with him, give her marriage another chance."

"And her husband has no idea about this man?"

"No. To be honest, as far as he's concerned, they don't have any problems."

"I hate to say it, but he's going to have a real eye-opener after hearing this."

"You can't possibly tell him. What if Emily shows up in the morning after breaking it off with this guy, to come back to Mark? If you tell him, their marriage will be over for sure."

"What if she doesn't come home? What if this man has her or worse? I'm sorry to be so harsh, but we have to look at the big picture. Unfortunately, without a name or description, my hands are tied."

"Wait a minute." She stood. "I remember what his vehicle looked like. Would that help?"

"It's better than nothing," he said, when in reality their conversation was at a standstill.

"It was a dark-colored SUV."

"Make? Model?"

She shook her head. "Sorry."

"Okay, Ms. Fellows, is that everything you came to tell me?"

"I know it's not much, but I thought you should know."

"I appreciate the information. Every little bit helps." He went to the door, opened it and walked her back down the hall. "If you remember anything more, or hear from Emily, please call me directly." He handed her his business card.

"Thank you, Detective."

Johnny went back to his office, brewed a pot of strong coffee, then opened the folder on his desk. As he leafed through the husband's responses to the standard questions, Johnny tried conjuring up an image of the woman before turning the page to look at the recent picture given to the police.

His whole body broke out in a sweat.

Just as he thought, the image he'd fabricated in his mind from the descriptions given by her husband and parents was nothing close to the woman's true identity. One's description was never the same as another, and that's why the picture itself was of utmost importance.

Auburn hair turned out to be that of your classic brunette. Even the eye color in the picture would beg to differ against the bluish green characteristic given by Emily Beth Harris's husband. Johnny shut his eyes in shock for a moment. It wasn't the lack of information that had him so troubled. It was the woman's picture, those eyes, her hair, even the shape of her face.

If his own wife hadn't been dead, he would have sworn Lindsey's eyes were staring back at him as he looked down at the picture. The similarities of the missing woman and Johnny's dead wife were *that* profound. Or was it his recent loss that made this girl appear so much like Lindsey?

His cell phone began to ring, but the sound seemed distant. The eyes of the picture still held him captive. The aching guilt of Lindsey's death reemerged. He let his cell ring, waited for it to stop. Eventually it did, the rapid beating of his heart in tune with the loud ticking of the clock the only sounds within the office.

The walls felt as though they were closing in on him, flashes from the past bouncing off all four. Lindsey, Tess, Lindsey, Tess, Emily Harris, Lindsey...

"Detective Sawyer? Are you still in there?" Officer Reinhold's voice exploded from the intercom.

Johnny didn't move, his body stiff, hands clammy, but managed to find the words, "Yeah, I'm here." He never once took his eyes from the picture below.

"There's a woman on the phone asking for you. She seems a bit hysterical, said her name was Tess."

His heart lurched. He snapped out of the trance, the red flashing bulb on the phone demanding his attention. Without responding to his messenger through the intercom, Johnny snatched up the phone, stuffing the picture of Emily Harris back into the folder.

"Tess, what's the matter? Are you okay?"

"Johnny, I'm scared."

He could hear her muffled sobs, the fear in her voice.

"Tell me what's wrong? Where are you?"

"I'm home...The phone calls, they wouldn't stop."

"What're you talking about? Slow down, what phone calls?"

"Someone was there, but they wouldn't say anything. I hung up."

"It was probably just a couple of kids making a random prank call." Johnny let out a sigh of relief.

"That's what I thought, too, but they called back..." Tess went silent, then whispered, "Johnny, I swear to God, the woman on the other end of the line... Lindsey... She sounded exactly like Lindsey."

Johnny moved his hand back to the manila case file. Without opening it, he slid a finger underneath the edge and slowly withdrew the picture. It was Emily's hair that he saw first, her forehead, her eyes... Those eyes. He jerked his hand back, pushing the chair from the desk, placing his hand to the cold metal lodged securely in his shoulder holster.

"Lock your doors, Tess. I'm on my way."

Chapter Seven

Lock your doors.

Johnny's words were seared in her head. Tess hung up the phone, checked both the front and back door, turning the deadbolts just to be safe. Her panic took her from room to room, making sure every window was also locked.

It wasn't until she was making her way back down the stairs that she realized something odd about her conversation with Johnny. It was as if he had known. Not necessarily about the phone calls but about the daunting voice of the caller.

He hadn't argued with Tess about hearing Lindsey's voice. It couldn't have been her voice, Tess reassured herself, grounding her sanity before she went mad. If anything, she'd half expected Johnny to hang up on her, thinking she was nuts from the second the words left her lips.

Yet he hadn't. He'd been quiet, maybe even shocked, but he hadn't argued with her.

Tess stopped halfway down the stairs and took a seat, the front door in view, the driveway beyond the slender windows on either side of the door empty.

"Come on, Johnny, hurry up." Tess pulled her knees to her chest, wrapping her arms tightly around them.

The last thing she wanted to be doing was turning to Johnny, asking for his help. She had tried to remain calm, to rationalize the situation after hearing the familiar voice, but it had been impossible. After she had hung up on the caller, her phone kept ringing and ringing.

She hadn't been able to take it any more. Not knowing his home phone number, she had finally decided to try Johnny at the station. She felt like such a crazy fool, bringing all of this madness involving his dead wife back into his life just when...

Just when he seemed to finally be moving on.

She rubbed her arms but nothing took away the coldness from her bones. She looked down the stairs, toward her living room. The reflection of flames from within the fireplace bounced off the walls, the memories of herself and Johnny came rushing back.

His lips on hers, the way he'd so tenderly caressed every inch of her body, the way they had made love as if the years apart never existed. His confession, her anger overwhelming her pain, Johnny walking away.

The phone rang.

Tess jumped. "Damn it, Johnny, where are you?"

It continued to ring until the machine picked up. For the second time that night she heard Johnny's voice coming through the machine.

"Tess, I'm just pulling up your driveway." She saw the headlights, watched as the vehicle stopped and Johnny stepped out. "All right, Tess, I'm here. Open up."

She ran down the stairs and straight to the door, not able to stop from looking through the peephole. She sighed. He was there. Finally, he was there.

Without wasting any more time, she flung open the door

and threw herself into his arms. It wasn't until he wrapped her tight, held her close, that she realized how scared she had been. Now she was safe, safe in Johnny's arms. Safe in his *trembling* arms.

Had he been that terrified for her well-being?

Of course he had. Lindsey's loss was still fresh in his mind. How could she have been so insensitive? When calling the station, she should have reported the phone calls to the answering officer instead of asking for Johnny. But what would she have told them? That the wife of Detective Sawyer was harassing her from the grave?

No, they would've thought she was crazy.

Whether it brought back his pain or not, Johnny was the only person Tess could talk to about this. Except he wasn't talking. Anyone else, put in these circumstances, would've questioned her by now, yet Johnny remained silent with no apparent intentions of letting her go.

Tess pulled back and gazed into his eyes.

"I'm sorry I called you. I know this must sound crazy, but I could've sworn it was—"

"Come on, let's go inside."

Tess went first and Johnny followed, closing the door behind him, shutting out the first signs of morning light. It was hard to believe that mere hours ago they had put all their problems aside, forgotten about the past and had spent a wonderful evening alone by the fire. Now this. The fact that their reunion had been cut short because of a resurfacing lie would only make it harder for them to sort through the mess.

"I want you to start from the beginning, tell me everything about these calls. When was the first, did they speak when you answered, was there more than one person who you talked to?"

"There's not much to tell. Like I said, the first call was silent."

"But you thought you heard someone on the line?" Johnny asked.

"I did. I pressed mute, hoping they would think I hung up. That's when I heard the breathing. I listened, but the person didn't speak, so I hung up."

"How many calls were there?" Johnny asked.

"One more."

Just the thought of it caused chills to take over her body. Who would play such a sick joke on her?

"What did they say?"

"It wasn't *they*, Johnny, it was a woman, a woman who sounded a hell of a lot like Lindsey."

"That's impossible."

"I know, but it doesn't make it any less unnerving."

She stood, staring, trying to read him, trying to figure out what was going through his head. Why hadn't she noticed earlier how much he had changed? His easygoing nature as a boy was now replaced with complexity, tension, all the traits of a man who had lived a rough life, survived a tragedy.

The chime of the clock demanded her attention. Six a.m. Tess hadn't had an ounce of sleep since Johnny had left during the early morning hours, and from the looks of him, neither had he.

"I'm going to go make some coffee, then we can sort through this." Tess started for the kitchen, hollering over her shoulder, "Make yourself at home."

"Wait a minute."

She turned to face him.

"You never answered my question. What did this woman say?"

"*You'll be sorry.*" With the answer to his question, she continued on to the kitchen, in desperate need of caffeine.

When she returned to the living room, she wasn't prepared to find Johnny sitting on the couch, a glass of whiskey in hand, the bottle between his legs. She looked into the dining room at the lower glass cupboard of the china hutch. It had been a long time since she'd had a dinner party—she had forgotten all about the half-empty bottle of whiskey.

Again she looked at the clock. What was he thinking, drinking this early in the morning? She set down the coffee tray on a nearby end table and went to stand before him. She glared at him, then toward the bottle, but his response only angered her further. He brought the glass to his lips and swallowed its contents in one neat tip of his hand.

"What're you doing?"

"You said to make myself at home."

"If I knew you were going to drink yourself into a stupor, I would've had *you* make the coffee." Tess reached down, taking hold of the whiskey bottle, but Johnny latched on to her wrist.

"Leave it." He waited until she let go before releasing her arm, then proceeded to refill his glass. "After you hear what I have to tell you, believe me, you'll be pouring yourself a drink, too."

Something in his voice told Tess he wasn't kidding.

"What're you talking about?"

"Get yourself a cup of coffee." Johnny nodded to the tray across the room. "Then sit down."

Tess walked back to the tray and did as she was told. She picked up the carafe and filled the black mug, never taking her gaze from Johnny as he sipped away at the whiskey. Aware of her intent, judgmental glare, he set the glass on the table and waited for her to join him on the couch.

However, Tess didn't have any intentions of sitting next to him. No. Forcing Johnny to let her by, she removed the whiskey bottle and took a seat in front of him on the coffee table.

"Why don't you seem surprised about that phone call?" Tess held his gaze until Johnny diverted his stare. "What aren't you telling me?"

Johnny sat up in his seat, removed his coat and pulled a file from the back of his pants. He laid it on the table next to Tess, then reclaimed the glass of whiskey before leaning back on the couch.

She glanced down.

The file had the Dawson Valley Police logo imprinted along the front. A white sticker on the top right-hand corner read Emily Harris. Tess was confused. It wasn't until then that she remembered she had found Johnny at the police station.

Had their earlier confrontation sent him there in an attempt to clear his head, to catch up on unfinished work, or had he been called in on a case? Had this file containing information on this Emily Harris person been the reason for Johnny being at the station in the middle of the night?

What did it have to do with Tess?

If there was one thing she'd learned, having worked for a law firm all these years, it was that under no circumstances was she ever to talk about the details of the many cases she was privy to. The same rule went for cops, and surely applied to the head detective in a case.

What is in that file, and why is Johnny offering the information to me?

As if reading her mind, he said, "Go ahead. Take a look."

"You want me to open it? Isn't this confidential?" The black stamp on the front of the file said as much.

"Yes."

"I don't understand." Tess picked up the file, holding it with both hands, using her left thumb to flip the folder open, but Johnny's hand came down hard, slapping it into her lap before she saw what was inside. "What're you doing? I thought you wanted me to look at this."

"I do, but I have to warn you... What you see inside must never leave this room." He tapped the file. "I could get in a world of shit if it ever got out."

"Of course."

"One more thing. The picture you are about to see... Don't freak out on me."

With a statement like that, Tess half expected to find some gruesome crime-scene photo within the file, but what she found staring back at her was worse. She dropped the folder and jumped to her feet, knocking over the whiskey bottle in the process.

"What kind of sick joke are you trying to pull!" she snapped, giving a sideward glance to the fallen bottle, its contents seeping onto the carpet. "I knew I should've never called you. I'd expect something like this from that asshole partner of yours, but you..."

"Tess, calm down."

"Calm down? Don't freak out? I see what this is about. You're pissed that I walked away from you earlier and think I have nothing better to do than make up stories about a dead woman calling me in order to get back at you, to hurt you. Damn it, Johnny, this isn't funny!"

Johnny stood, the look in his eyes warning her that his words were going to be far from understanding.

"You better hold it right there. If you think this is about you and me, you're highly mistaken. I don't have the time for games, Tess." Johnny bent down and picked up the papers, locating the picture, holding it inches from her face. "The woman in this photo, her husband reported her missing a couple of hours ago. I was as shocked as you to see her resemblance to Lindsey. But that's all it is. My wife is dead, I buried her, and I can't believe you would think I'd use that to get to you. Don't flatter yourself."

His callous words ripped at Tess's heart.

"I didn't mean it," was all she could say.

"Yes, you did."

"Can you blame me?" Tess tore the picture from his grasp, giving it a closer look. "This woman, she's a spitting image of Lindsey. This is crazy!"

"At least I know I'm not going crazy," he said underneath his breath then looked at Tess. "It's the timing of it all. This report, that phone call you received... Someone's trying to mess with me."

"Why would they call me?"

"Maybe someone saw us together at the restaurant. I don't know who or why someone would go through this kind of trouble to get to me. It's sick."

"What if they saw you here, when you picked me up?"

Suddenly the image of the SUV prowling in front of her house the evening before seemed relevant to all the madness. Were the man behind the wheel and the woman in Johnny's case file connected?

"There's something I should tell you."

"If it's more babbling about you, me and our sordid past, I don't want to hear it." Johnny dismissed her and went to pick up the empty whiskey bottle. "Do you have something to clean this up?"

"Leave it." She took the bottle from his hand and set it on the tray containing the coffee. "Aren't you the least bit interested in what I have to say?"

"After the night I've had, I don't think there's anything that would surprise me."

"Remember when you called, before dinner, and the machine picked up?"

"Yeah. So?"

"I told you I was upstairs, couldn't get to the phone. When you came to the door, I screamed when you rang the bell."

"I don't need a play-by-play of something that's already happened, Tess."

"You asked me if something was wrong," she continued, regardless of Johnny's lack of interest.

"And you told me you were fine. Let me see..." Johnny rubbed at his chin. "Something about the doorbell startling you. No, wait, you blamed it on being hungry."

"I lied." Although Johnny was using sarcasm as a means of dealing with the fact that there was a woman running around out there with Lindsey's face, Tess was scared. "I lied."

"What do you mean you lied?" Johnny asked.

She had his attention now.

She went to the front window. "Before you called, I thought I had seen your SUV parked out front." She moved the lace curtain back a bit. "I was sure it was you sitting out there, waiting for me."

"I didn't park in the street." Johnny was directly behind

115

her. "I pulled up your driveway, remember?"

"Of course. You didn't let me finish." Tess turned around to face him. "The SUV, parked in the street... I was ready to go out the door, to meet you at the curb, but then the vehicle's interior light came on. That's when I realized it wasn't you."

"Who the hell was it?"

"I don't know, but he was looking right at me. I couldn't see his face. He was wearing a baseball hat low on his forehead. It creeped me out, as though he knew me, knew exactly where I was standing even though I tried to stay hidden. Then you called. In the time I took to answer the phone and return to the window, he was gone."

"Are you sure it was a man?" Johnny asked.

"Yes."

"Dear God."

"What?" His concern proved she had made the right decision in telling him about the strange visitor. "What is it?"

"I remember seeing taillights fading down the street when I arrived, but I didn't think anything of it."

"Why would you?"

Johnny went back to the coffee table and picked up the folder, rifling madly through the papers until he found what he was looking for.

"Tess?" Johnny pulled out a document, then made the few short steps to her side. "Do you remember the make of the SUV? The color?"

"I can't tell you for sure what kind of vehicle it was, but the color... It was dark. Not black, though." Tess once again looked out the window, concentrating, envisioning the man out front, her insides trembling at the thought. She turned back to Johnny. "Dark. I'm almost positive it was a dark color."

"I'll be damned."

"Do you know who it was?" She prayed he did.

"No, but I'm more convinced than ever that someone's trying to mess with me, and they're using you and my job to do it."

"What would someone have to gain by doing that?"

"I don't know, but you can bet I'm going to find out."

Johnny walked to the couch to get his jacket, along the way grabbing the black button-up shirt from the back of the chair, the one he had left at Tess's that night.

"Where are you going?"

After their recent findings, the last thing Tess wanted was to be left alone, but was it any safer to be depending on Johnny for protection?

"Home." He pulled out his cell phone but before dialing out, said, "Pack a bag. You're going with me."

"But—"

Johnny held up a hand to silence her. "This is not debatable. Get your things and let's go."

Chapter Eight

Tess was tired, confused and found herself in quite a predicament. She had done as Johnny asked—more like demanded—and was packed and ready to go in twenty minutes. While she had been upstairs, she had heard Johnny on his cell phone but hadn't been able to make out the conversation. When she emerged in the living room, he was pacing at the front door, making her feel as though she'd taken too long.

"Are you ready?" He pulled out his keys with his right hand, the file in the left.

"I'm not leaving this house until you tell me why the color of that SUV was so important."

She hadn't wanted to be left alone after seeing the picture in the file, talking about the stranger at her house, but going home with Johnny? Was it really necessary?

"Let me worry about that. Now, come on." He opened the front door and stepped out on the porch.

Tess didn't follow, bringing Johnny back through the door in no time flat.

"I told you I'm not leaving."

"Some things never change."

"What's that supposed to mean?" She put defiant hands on her hips.

"Now's not the time to be stubborn. If you'll get in the damn vehicle I'll explain everything."

"You better, Johnny, because—"

"Now's not the time to be making threats, either."

She wanted to scream but knew the sooner she gave in, the sooner she'd get answers. They walked out together. Tess locked up, and Johnny double-checked to be sure.

Tess couldn't get over his attitude. This was the first she'd seen of the bitter man he'd become. How foolish she'd been to think that one night back in his arms would change everything. They might have been able to get through the secrets of the past, but this new case he was dealing with, one she found herself involved in, was already taking its toll on him.

They drove in silence. Johnny wasn't making an effort to divulge the promised information, but Tess couldn't wait any longer. If she was being taken from her house because of this case, she had a right to know the details. Confidential or not.

"All right, 'fess up. I think you owe me an explanation." She expected more silence.

"I said I'd tell you, didn't I?"

"Out with it. I'm assuming it has something to do with why you're taking me with you? Am I in danger?" The thought was unsettling.

"I'm not sure, but I'm not taking any chances." He stopped for a red light. "I can't."

One minute Tess found herself furious with him, in the next she had nothing but sympathy. She realized why Johnny wanted her to go with him. He still blamed himself for Lindsey's death and probably felt obligated to protect Tess. She didn't want it to be like this, wanted Johnny to *want* to be with her, but not because he feared for her life.

"You're pretty quiet for a woman on a mission."

"What does that SUV have to do with the woman in the picture?"

"Her sister showed up at the station after the husband and the rest of the family left, claiming Emily Harris had been having an affair no one but her knew about."

"You don't think she's missing, do you?"

"Not any more." Johnny drove past the house he had shared with Lindsey, noticing the question on Tess's face. "I sold the place after she died, bought a house out in the middle of nowhere."

Tess took in the sight of the house, different now than it had been when they had rented it as kids. It saddened her, thinking back on all the times they had shared. Good and bad. All the love, the heartache, the price they had paid for falling in love so young, so fast.

"How do you like living in the country?" Tess asked, wanting to rid her mind of the old pain.

"It suits me." He removed a pair of black sunglasses from the visor. "Anyway, back to Emily Harris. Her sister doesn't know who this guy is that Emily's been sleeping with, doesn't know what he looks like, just that he drives a dark-colored SUV."

"You think this guy and the one who was at my house are the same person?"

"I know he is. And Emily Harris... I think she's the one who called you. By the way, I'm having a tap put on your phone. We'll be able to trace the number the minute your machine picks up."

"I don't understand any of this. Do you know this woman?"

"Never heard of her."

"I can't believe how much she looks like Lindsey." Tess shook her head in sheer amazement.

"Yeah, it's like seeing a ghost."

Johnny took a left on a dirt road. He wasn't kidding when he said he bought a place in the middle of nowhere. It had been years since Tess had been down this road, and when Johnny pulled up to his house, she remembered exactly how long.

"Is this...?"

"You remembered." He shut off the engine and reached in the backseat to collect her things.

"How could I forget?"

Johnny had brought Tess to the abandoned farmhouse on many occasions during the first couple of months into their relationship. One particular night stood out from the rest.

Tess had told her parents she was staying with a friend, ironically Lindsey. She and Johnny had packed a bag and driven out to this very house, as always sneaking in through a back window. She remembered the first gleam of candlelight as she walked into the large dining area and saw a tent pitched in the middle of the room.

She recalled how she had laughed at the sight of the tent in the house, but Johnny had quickly reminded her of the many critters that called the empty place their home. She hadn't been scared. Not with Johnny by her side.

They had made love for the first time that night, and now Tess was back, back with the man who had taken more than her virginity. He had taken her heart.

"So what do you think?" Johnny asked, leading her up the cobblestone path.

"I don't remember the place looking like this." Tess couldn't believe her eyes. "Did you do all the work?"

"Most of it. Mike helped."

"It's beautiful."

Tess admired the manicured lawn, remembering back to the way it had looked before, patches of grass here and there, practically high enough to have been considered a field. He'd had the old shingles of the house replaced with stained cedar ones. Country blue shutters topped off its uniqueness.

How appropriate. She grinned.

Johnny stood on the front porch, the shadows of a faint smile on his lips, watching her take in the sight.

"If you think this looks good—" Johnny tapped the railing before him, "—wait till you see the inside."

Tess couldn't wait. This was exactly what she needed to keep her mind off what was going on around them. Like a kid, she raced up the front steps and waited by Johnny's side with anticipation as he opened the front door.

"Wow," she said in awe. It looked like a totally different house. "May I?"

"Make yourself at home." Johnny motioned for Tess to move forward. "Just don't raid my liquor cabinet."

"Not everyone enjoys a whiskey at six a.m."

As she moved farther into the house, Tess noticed the huge sunken living room to her left. Johnny had always had a knack for making things look perfect, even though he would never admit to being a good decorator. He'd say that was a woman's job.

She slowly descended the two shallow steps and walked across the dark blue carpet. The furnishings were very masculine. A black leather sectional was aligned against the back wall, continuing under the front bay window. The matching leather recliner stood off by itself with a perfect view of the television set, typically suited for a male.

Johnny wasn't around, and Tess took it upon herself to complete the tour alone. There was one room she wanted to see more than any other. She headed to the back of the house, turning her head from left to right, taking in every detail of Johnny's new life, passing a small bathroom, an office, decorated with plaques and framed awards from Johnny's time on the Force.

Then she stopped, speechless by the room before her.

She stepped through the archway, gazing about the dining room in confusion. Other than the room having been cleaned, it had been completely untouched. The wallpaper, the old plank-board floors, the hutch, the long table, every detail was as Tess remembered, as if she had walked backward in time.

"If I had known you were coming, I would've put up a tent for you." For the first time since holding her in his arms, Johnny showed some real compassion. "Remember, we used to set it up right here." He went to the back corner of the room.

"How could I forget." Tess remembered. Boy, did she ever remember. As her eyes continued to scan the room, one question remained. "Why'd you keep it like this?"

"Just haven't gotten around to changing it."

Tess found his explanation to be nothing more than an excuse, seeing as he had renovated the rest of the downstairs, yet she didn't challenge him further, didn't ask him why the windowsill in the far corner still held the stick candles from eleven years ago.

Johnny's gaze was upon her now. She could feel it. He knew what she was looking at, the candles, which had been their only source of light as young lovers. Could he possibly be feeling the same emotions of the past that were tearing at Tess's heart? She needed to know.

"I find it strange that you redid this entire house, except for this room," Tess said, hoping he would open up.

"Come on, let's go out back." He walked past her, totally disregarding her assumption. "Don't tell me you forgot about the pond?"

"The pond..." Tess smiled.

Together they made their way around the side of the house. Tess noticed Johnny had remodeled the once worn, fallen-down side porch, and had added a deck on the back. It was clear he had kept busy after Lindsey's death, which made Tess wonder if he had given himself time to grieve.

"Here we are."

"Amazing." The view took her breath away.

Johnny's backyard consisted of a glorious jade green meadow speckled with an array of fuchsia, violet and navy blue wildflowers. Directly in the center was a small pond decorated with lily pads to accommodate the many types of wildlife that called the pond their home.

"Still looks the same after all these years." Johnny led Tess into the meadow.

"Just like I remember."

"We spent a lot of time here."

"Can you believe we carried all these stones from over the hill and put them around that edge of the pond?" Tess walked to the other end of the small pool, thinking back on an easier time where there were no stalkers, no eerie voices, no tension between her and Johnny.

"We made quite the team, didn't we?"

"Yeah, we did." She knelt down at the water's edge.

She wished she could turn back the hands of time. She would have done things differently and was almost positive that

Johnny would've, too.

The water was as clear as could be, with plenty of activity going on below the surface. Salamanders were swimming leisurely without a care in the world. Polliwogs were showing the first signs of maturing into frogs, little legs beginning to form from the end of their bodies.

Tess ran her hand along the top of the grass that bordered the bank of the pond. Some things never changed... Anxious frogs jumped into the water for fear of being caught by human hands.

Tess stood, turned and faced Johnny.

"Did you used to bring Lindsey here, too?" Somehow she couldn't help but mention the past.

"No." Johnny shook his head, the sadness apparent in his eyes.

"I'm sorry." She hadn't meant to bring up Lindsey, but being at that house, in that meadow, had sucked Tess right back in time.

Johnny held up a hand to halt her from saying anything further, as if begging her to let it go.

Tess left him at the edge of the pond and walked to the outer edge of the meadow, wondering if the names were still engraved in the mammoth maple tree. She remembered how deep Johnny had carved the letters.

Making a path through the tall grass, she approached the third tree, slowly lifted her gaze to its trunk. There it was. A little worn from the weather but still legible. *Johnny Sawyer and Tess Fenmore.*

They had been so young. Johnny had torn into that tree like a pro. For hours he had sat there, making sure each and every letter was neat.

She lifted her fingers to touch the outline as she had done before, after he had finished his work of art. If only it were possible to go back in time, just for one day, but that wasn't practical thinking.

Being back in this meadow did more for her than simply reestablish the happy childhood memories. It scared her. No matter how much she denied it, she was still more in love with Johnny than she could have ever thought possible.

How could she go on with her life and be truly happy without him in it? She wanted to finish their conversation from the night before, wished she hadn't hidden in her bathroom like a coward. She had questions about how Johnny had felt back then, about his marriage to Lindsey, about how he felt now.

Tess glanced over her shoulder, doubting her courage. Johnny was slowly approaching her, his thoughts, like hers, weighing heavily on his face.

She should have been grateful he had joined her by the tree. This place wasn't complete without the two of them there together. After the events of the last twenty-four hours, they had both created emotional walls to protect their hidden feelings, and Tess wasn't sure if she had the strength to let hers down.

"You're right, you know?" Johnny sat in the grass and glanced up at Tess.

"Right about what?"

His statement had thrown her off guard, and she wasn't certain what he was implying.

"I should've fought harder for you." He rubbed at his jawline as if deep in thought, scuffing his fingers against the stubble on his face. "Like I said, things were different then, and we can't go back."

"No, we can't, but I think if we talk about it, we can make

things right." Tess was willing to try if Johnny was. "I want to know about you, about the last eleven years of your life."

"What's there to tell? I went into the police academy, became a cop. I was married, now I'm not."

He wasn't making this easy on her.

"Tell me about your marriage." Talking about Lindsey might give Johnny some closure and, at the same time, give her some acceptance.

He hesitated for a moment. "We were married for nine years."

"That's a long time."

"Yeah, it was." Johnny plucked a tall blade of grass from the ground. "And the last couple of years... Well, it doesn't matter now."

"You must have been happy."

"There's so much you don't know, and I'm not even sure it's worth stirring up at this point." Johnny tore the blade of grass in half, then tossed it to the side. "Lindsey's dead, and I can't change what became of our marriage, just wish I could make sense of it."

"The last thing I want to do is rehash the past again, but I can tell something's eating away at you. Whether it was something you did, something Lindsey did, I don't know, but sooner or later it's going to take over you." She had crossed the line. His gaze told her as much. However, she had come this far. There was no sense in holding back now. "Johnny... About last night, what happened between us—"

"It should've never happened." He stood. "It won't happen again. I brought you here to keep you safe, and that's about all I can handle right now."

Tess stomped after Johnny, following him into the house.

"This hot and cold attitude of yours really stinks," she said, blown away by his dismissal.

"If you don't mind..." He yawned, tilting his neck from side to side, a nervous habit that had never ceased. "I've probably had all of five minutes of sleep in the last thirty-six hours. I called the station, told them I'd be working from home today. After I get a couple of hours of sleep, I plan on thoroughly going over that case file."

"That's all you have to say?"

"That's all I care to say." Johnny left the dining room and Tess followed him into the kitchen. "Want something to eat before I head upstairs?"

"I couldn't eat if I wanted to."

Once again, Johnny Sawyer had managed to sting her with hurtful words. More than ever, Tess regretted having called him for help. If he had brought her to his home out of obligation, to ease his lingering guilt, she didn't want his kind of help.

"Suit yourself. When you're ready, you can rest in the spare room upstairs, second door on the right." Johnny headed up the back stairwell, off the kitchen, pulling his shirt over his head as he disappeared out of sight.

CB

Johnny went to his room but sleep didn't come easy. Too many factors to too many lives were in his hands, Tess's being at the top of his list.

He had made a mistake. He should've never taken her to dinner, never given in to the temptation of being with her again. The guilt had briefly subsided during the last few months, not forgotten, rather locked away in the depths of his mind, enabling him to get back on his feet again.

Now it was back in full force. Every time he looked at Tess, he felt the blame for having hurt her, every time he talked to Mike, all they did was fight. He found himself snapping at everyone these days.

And worst of all, Johnny thought, sitting in the recliner by the window, opening the file in his hand, he felt the guilt of Lindsey's death escalate every time he looked at Emily Harris's face.

Why was this happening to him just when he had finally put it all to rest?

Then there was the extra pressure of keeping Tess safe... Although the man had only appeared to her once, Johnny had to wonder how many other times he had gone unnoticed. Had he followed her home from work? Had he been in her home? The question that scared Johnny most—was he someone Tess knew and trusted?

The cop in him imagined circumstance after circumstance, but nothing helped. He needed to catch this guy. Once he did, he would find Emily Harris. He was sure of it. And if he happened upon Emily first, Johnny would make her lead him to this man. Either way, he was going to find out why these two people were harassing Tess and what they wanted from him.

For now Tess was at his house, the one place where he knew she'd be safe. He would keep her here as long as he saw fit, as long as she would stay.

Johnny couldn't allow their relationship—or lack thereof— to cloud his judgment, to distract him from the dangers beyond his home. No matter how much he wanted to let her in, tell her his true feelings, he had to keep her at arm's length. And under no circumstances could he ever let himself get as close to her as he had the previous night in front of her fireplace.

Her safety, his sanity, the case of Emily Harris's

disappearance... They all depended on it.

Cℨ

She waited a while before following Johnny upstairs, sitting at the kitchen table, staring out at the picturesque view through the gleaming bay window, feeling anything but comfortable in his home.

She wished she had insisted on driving her car, but Johnny probably wouldn't have gone for that, knowing she could up and leave whenever she wanted. How long did he expect her to stay, surely no longer than tonight? There was her job to think about, her family.

Her dad would want to know why she was staying with Johnny, and she couldn't very well tell him the truth. It would scare him to death, the idea of someone stalking his only daughter. He would insist on her coming home to be with him and her mother.

As far as Tess was concerned, that was not an option.

Her eyelids were dropping. She was exhausted. She couldn't fight the drowsiness any longer. Pushing the chair from the table, Tess stood, stretched, looking at the entrance that led to the second floor.

Which door had Johnny said was to the spare bedroom? She tried replaying his instructions in her mind but was still reeling from his hurtful words. Was it the first door on the right or the second? She couldn't be sure, was almost tempted to go into the living room and lie on the couch.

She braved forward, through the archway, retracing Johnny's steps, listening for the slightest clue as to which room was his. Nothing. Not a snore, no heavy breathing, nothing, and both doors were closed.

She reached for the handle and opened the first door on the right. She peeked in and saw an empty bed. She let out a sigh of relief, pushed open the door and stepped into the room. It was the squeaking of the door that grabbed her attention first, but it was Johnny, sleeping in the chair, that froze her to the ground, hoping, praying she hadn't woken him.

He didn't move. He lay there, sound asleep, having given in to the stress of the hours before. Tess wanted to run, to make her escape before being detected, yet she couldn't pull her gaze from him.

He had reclined the chair, had taken the time to kick off his shoes, but appeared uncomfortable. His face was that of a troubled man, Emily Harris's case file spread open across his lap.

She wanted to go to him, wanted to pick up that damn file and throw it out the window, along with all of their problems, old and new, lock the doors to the world outside and never look back. That had been her problem all along, the same one that had affected her life up until this point.

Always looking back.

Johnny could deny his feeling all he wanted, but there was no way he could have faked what they had shared the night before, the way he'd touched her, the words he had whispered almost breathlessly in her ear. She had to believe he couldn't be that cruel.

He started to stir, and the last thing she wanted was for him to find her staring at him. She took two steps back, closing the door as she left, the squeak almost silent this time. She kept on down the hallway, then entered the second room on the right.

She approached the bed and sat, wishing she had brought her overnight bag upstairs with her. Her cotton shorts would've been a lot more comfortable than the jeans she had on. She looked at the door. No lock. What the heck was she afraid of? They were both adults.

Rising from the bed, Tess unbuttoned her jeans and tugged them past her hips. Sitting back down, using one foot to assist the other, she kicked off her jeans and climbed beneath the comforter. Eyes heavy against the feather pillow, exhaustion took over, carrying her away from her problems and off to a troubled sleep.

Chapter Nine

Johnny could've stood in the doorway forever watching Tess sleep, the length of her shirt barely covering her backside. He had slept for four hours and probably could've slept for another four if it hadn't been for the disturbing ringing of his cell phone.

Against Johnny's orders, Mark Harris had come back, demanding to know why the Dawson Valley P.D. wasn't doing more to find his wife. The Chief was out of town, the on-duty officers were all on calls, the new woman tending to the switchboard was overwhelmed and his partner was nowhere to be found.

He needed to get to the station but didn't want to leave Tess. He walked to the side of the bed and reached out, almost touched her bare arm, but restrained himself. The less contact they had, the better. It took everything in him not to strip himself of his clothes and climb in next to her.

He had brought Tess there for one reason and one reason only, he reminded himself—to keep her safe. He wasn't going to take the chance of that creep getting close to her again. The tricky part was going to be convincing Tess his house was where she needed to be.

She was so damn stubborn.

Looking at his watch, he realized he didn't have time to wait for Tess to get up. Even if he woke her now, by the time she got ready Mark Harris would have the station in shambles. He had to leave.

Johnny assessed the house, double-checking to make sure everything was locked, set the security alarm as an extra precaution and left Tess with a note on the nightstand in the room where she still slept.

 C3

Tess walked through the fog toward the silhouette standing at the end of the driveway. Calling out to him was pointless—the sound of thunder crashed through the air. She longed to be held by him, yet picking up her pace didn't bring her any closer. It was as though she were traveling through an endless tunnel. She stopped, waving her arms in the air. Her effort to be seen seemed to bring him close, closer... He was now in front of her, facing her, touching her. Suddenly, she froze. Standing before her wasn't Johnny, but the man who had lurked outside her house the day before. Once again his face was concealed.

"You can't hide from me, Tess," he roared over the thunder, the night sky flashing in the distance. She turned and ran as fast as her legs would carry her. She could still hear his haunting laughter and was unable to escape the sound. She hit a brick wall. Again he was before her, two inches from her face.

"Johnny promised to protect you, but look at you now, here, all alone with no one to save you from my grasp." His hands were at her throat, slowly squeezing the life out of her...

From a dead sleep, Tess sat straight up, trying to register her surroundings. Johnny's. She was at Johnny's. Her mind was playing awful tricks on her. What a nightmare. How had her life gotten out of control, so fast?

She had only seen the stranger in the SUV once. For all she knew he could've mistaken her house for someone else's. Maybe she was being paranoid for nothing. Even so, that didn't explain the mysterious phone call, the sound of Lindsey's voice haunting her from the grave.

Regardless of repeated attempts to make sense of the situation, Johnny seemed to think it warranted Tess leaving her home to stay under his watchful eye. For now, Tess had no choice but to trust him.

She wished there weren't so much tension between them, wished they would've moved forward as a couple after helplessly giving in to their desire the night before. That would have been the perfect ending to their overdue reunion, after spending years apart, unaware of the other's feelings kept bottled up inside.

But she wasn't naïve. She knew there was no way to lock up the past and throw away the key. They weren't kids any more, and they both had their issues. Staying with Johnny might very well protect her from the stalker, if that's what that man was, but how was she going to protect herself from Johnny hurting her all over again?

One minute he was opening up, then in the next he was taking two steps back, pushing her away. Tess looked at her watch. It was already midafternoon, and she had slept most of the day away. As she sat up, she noticed the white sheet of paper on the nightstand.

There was an emergency at the station. Help yourself to anything in the kitchen. Don't open the doors for anyone, and whatever you do, do NOT leave this house. Be back when I can. ~Johnny

"Great." Tess crunched up the note and threw it across the

room.

Not only had she agreed to come to Johnny's against her better judgment, he had made her a prisoner in his home. His justification for bringing her there was to keep an eye on her. Why hadn't he woken her up?

Tess threw her legs over the side of the bed, letting out a grumble. She was annoyed. It wasn't as though she'd expected Johnny to ignore his duties as a detective, but she thought he would have had the decency to let her know what was going on. Not leave her a note filled with orders. She could've gone with him, he could've dropped her off at her house while he worked, anything but keep her locked up out in the middle of nowhere.

When Johnny returned, Tess planned to tell him exactly what was on her mind. This was her life, and no man, not even Johnny Sawyer, was going to try to control it. No matter what the consequence.

Sure enough, when she reached the bottom of the stairs, the house was empty. She was tempted to call him, give him a piece of her mind, but she didn't want him to know he had gotten the best of her. Instead, she opened the refrigerator door and sighed.

A carton of expired milk, two containers of Chinese takeout, ketchup, mustard, one bottle of beer... How generous of him to tell her to help herself. He hadn't left her with much of a selection.

Tess reached in and opened the crisper, hoping to find the makings for a salad. Nothing. Other than the bottle of beer, there was nothing worth a second look.

With her hands on her hips, and her stomach growling, Tess began to weigh her options. She could sit there, waiting for Johnny to get back, hopefully with some groceries, or she could search out a phone book and order a pizza. Tess went to the phone and picked up, then slammed it back down.

"No, I'm not going to call to check when he'll be back."

This was crazy. His note said not to leave, not to answer the door. She knew Johnny meant well, but what harm could come from her ordering a darn pizza? She wasn't a child, for crying out loud, and she wasn't about to wait for him to come back empty-handed.

Without trying to be nosey, she began opening and closing drawers until she found the phone book. Before changing her mind, she dialed her favorite pizza parlor. When asked where the food was to be delivered, she had almost given the clerk her home address, then realized she wasn't even sure of Johnny's. She set the phone down and quickly peeked out the front door at the house number.

This guy on the phone must think I'm nuts.

She ran back inside, looking over her shoulder to make sure she had relocked the front door, then went into the kitchen.

"Seventy-six South Maple Drive."

She waited for her total, praying she had cash in her wallet, then hung up. Any other time, she would have been bothered to hear it would take forty-five minutes for the food to arrive, but she was grateful they would even deliver to a house this far out.

She went into the living room, found her overnight bag and promptly ran up the stairs. Since making love to Johnny and enduring the craziness that had followed, she hadn't had a moment's time to take a shower. If she hurried, she could freshen up before the food arrived.

Johnny had rushed her to pack, and she hadn't grabbed shampoo or soap. She'd been lucky to remember a toothbrush. She looked in the shower. His stuff would have to do. She shrugged.

She stepped in and gave her hair a good scrubbing, then washed from head to toe, the scent of Johnny's soap much stronger than she preferred. Very manly. Tess closed her eyes, letting the water wash over her body, hot on her skin, remembering the way Johnny smelled, the way his hands had felt on her body, tender, yet strong, truly amazing.

Steam filled the room, enveloping Tess in her memories, shutting out the world. She felt as though she could stay there forever. She tilted her head back, ran her fingers through her hair, then shut off the water.

She didn't have forever.

Just as she stepped out of the shower, the door to the bathroom flew open, leaving her standing there naked and in utter shock.

"Don't you know how to knock!" she screamed at Johnny.

"Damn it, Tess, you scared the hell out of me. I thought I told you to stay put!"

"What're you talking about? I haven't gone anywhere, couldn't if I wanted to! Where do you get off busting in here screaming at me?"

She reached for the towel, but it slid from the metal rack and fell to the floor. Johnny was instantly at her side, picking it up, wrapping it around her wet body, his hands warm against her skin. He held onto her shoulders, the anger in his eyes slowly fading, replaced with genuine affection.

"I'm sorry I yelled." He lessened his hold. "When I heard that the house alarm had gone off, I thought—"

"I didn't hear any alarm go off." Tess backed out of Johnny's hold and fastened the front of the towel.

"I set it before I left. When a door's opened, a silent alarm automatically goes to the security company and the station."

"It would've been nice if you had told me that." Tess reached for her bag. "You need to leave, so I can get dressed."

"Didn't you get my note?" he asked, ignoring her request.

"You mean the one ordering me to stay put? Yes, I got it. Now if you don't mind—"

"I do mind!"

She was grateful for everything Johnny was doing for her, but she was not a child, didn't appreciate being treated like one. If he thought he could stand there scolding her until she answered his questions, preventing her from getting dressed, Johnny was mistaken.

"Suit yourself."

The towel slid down her body and Johnny's gaze followed it to the floor. There she stood, naked, mere inches from his touch. They didn't speak and neither turned away, the idea of getting dressed now far from her mind. She wanted to press her body to him, force him to admit he wanted her as bad as she wanted him.

She took two steps forward, closing the gap between them. Placing her hands on his chest, his heart beating rapidly in time with hers, beneath her fingertips, Tess looked deep into his eyes, wanting nothing more than to feel his arms around her.

"Tess, stop." Johnny bent down to retrieve the towel.

"I know what you told me." She leaned in close, pulling him back up, her lips to his ear. "Why don't you do us both a favor and tell me how you really feel."

She could sense him breaking down, his body losing a battle his mind had fought hard to win. He leaned his head against hers, held her with the seriousness of his voice.

"I'm not going to lie to you. Being with you last night scared the hell out of me."

Tess opened her mouth to speak but was at a loss for words. She, too, knew how it felt to be scared.

"With all that's going on, I'm constantly on edge."

"I'm not looking for an apology, Johnny. Nobody expects you to save the world."

"Is that what you think I'm trying to do?" he asked, defensiveness returning in his tone.

"I don't think you know what you're doing half the time. You're so wrapped up in—"

His mouth swallowed her words, his barrier of resistance pushed to its limit. Tess closed her eyes to his touch, her body imploring him to never let her go. If only they could pick up where they had left off eleven years ago, leave all the pain behind.

"I don't want to do this to you. You'll just get hurt all over again."

Tess pulled away. "If you tell me right now that you don't ever want me this close to you again, touching you, kissing you..." Tess placed her lips softly to his shoulder. "Then I promise, I will leave and never look back."

"Leaving isn't an option, not until we find the man who's stalking you."

"You didn't answer my question. Like always, you're making this, us being together, about something else."

Suddenly, the doorbell sounded throughout the house. Tess held Johnny there, felt him tense up in her arms. There was a heavy rap on the door, ripping Johnny from the embrace, preventing Tess from getting the life-altering answer to her question.

She went to the doorway of the bathroom, holding the towel to her body, watched as Johnny ran down the main staircase on a rampage to get to the front door. Witnessing his reaction to the visitor on the other side frightened Tess, made her fully aware of how far gone Johnny was.

In two seconds flat, Johnny had the pizza on the ground and the delivery guy inside the house, against the wall, knocking off a picture in the process, glass shattering everywhere.

"Who the hell sent you here?" Johnny's fists clenched in the man's pin-striped shirt.

"Dude, calm down. I'm here to deliver a pizza." He held up his hands in surrender.

"Nobody ordered a damn pizza! You better start talking. Who sent you—"

"Johnny, stop it!" Tess screamed from halfway up the stairs. "I ordered the food! Let that boy go!"

Tess could see his anger reaching its peak as Johnny let go of the kid and focused on her. He stood glaring at Tess, emptying his lungs through a steady exhale. Johnny dug into his pocket and stuffed the cash in the hands of his victim.

"I apologize. Keep the change."

The deliveryman scurried out the door. Johnny waited until the car squealed out of the driveway, then slammed the door and looked at the mess of glass and pizza on the wood floor.

"What's the matter with you?" Tess made her way down the remaining steps. "I don't even know who you are any more."

"This is why the alarm went off," he said, more to himself than to Tess.

"Since when is it a crime to order a pizza?"

"I told you not to open the door for anyone! That's the same thing as asking someone to come to the house!"

He closed the gap between them.

Tess had had it, couldn't take the stress any longer. Johnny had gone over the edge, his emotions out of control.

"I'm going upstairs to get dressed, then you're taking me home."

She left him standing at the bottom of the stairs, tears streaming down her face as she went to collect her things. She had been wrong to think Johnny was on his way to recovering from issues surrounding Lindsey's death.

She had tried being there for him, had wanted to be much more to him, but she needed to accept there was nothing left for them. His life was so consumed with guilt, there was no room for Tess in it.

Dressed, her overnight bag in hand, Tess made her way down the hall, stopping briefly at Johnny's bedroom. Thinking back on the pain of the past couldn't compare to what she felt now, after a taste of what it could have been like for them in the future.

It wasn't as though she loved him any less, hell, she'd never loved him more, but he was out of her reach. The quicker she cut her ties with him, the better off they'd both be.

When she emerged through the kitchen stairwell, Johnny was seated at the table, the last beer from the fridge now empty. As their eyes met, Tess felt the ache inside cut deeper than ever before but knew they couldn't go on like this.

She had to be strong.

She needed to go home.

Chapter Ten

"Tess, put your bag down." Johnny gave her a sideward glance. "I didn't mean to go off on you."

"I appreciate that, but it doesn't change anything." Tess held her ground, not letting Johnny's sorry excuse for an apology suck her back in. "I want you to take me home."

"I don't think it's a good idea."

"Let's face it, Johnny, we don't even know if this guy's looking for me. He showed up at my house once, and I shouldn't have made a big deal about it. It's not as though he came to the door."

"Keep telling yourself that, maybe after a while you'll believe it." Johnny got up and went out the back door.

"Where are you going?" She pursued him.

Johnny sat on the top step of the deck, staring out at the pond.

"We heard from Emily Harris."

"You found her?" Tess set the bag down and went off the deck to stand in front of Johnny.

"Not exactly." He leaned back on both elbows, looking up at Tess. "I was called in to the station because her husband was there, demanding we continue the investigation even though he had heard from her hours before. Guess he didn't want to accept that she was leaving him for good."

"Is she okay?"

"I took a chance and called her cell. She answered. Her story corroborated her husband's. She apologized for our trouble, said she'd spent the night in a motel in the next town over, needed some time to sort through her problems."

"What about the guy in the SUV?" Tess felt relief for him that Emily had been found. Maybe now he could put the case of Lindsey's look-alike behind him.

"I tried my damnedest to get her to come in for questioning, but she wasn't ready for a run-in with her husband." Johnny massaged his neck muscles. "It's probably for the best. After seeing her resemblance to Lindsey, I don't know if I could've handled it."

"What about that guy, Johnny, is she with him?" Tess felt as though he was hiding something. Given the recent scene in the foyer, it would be just like him to take it all on his shoulders.

"She denied everything her sister told me, said there was no other man."

"None of this makes any sense. Why would her sister lie?"

"Unfortunately, this is typical of most domestic cases we deal with, and the shitty thing is there's not much more we can do. People call us, and we do our jobs by looking into each and every case, but in half the cases they waste our time."

"I have to ask..." Tess waited until Johnny met her gaze. "Her picture looked like Lindsey, did she sound like her, too?"

"No," Johnny said. "Not at all."

"How could this all be coincidental?" Tess felt the signs of a migraine threatening to explode in her head. "Someone called me last night. I didn't imagine that. If it wasn't Emily Harris, a woman who could pass for Lindsey's twin, then who the hell called and why?"

"I don't know what to make of it, could be someone's idea of a sick joke."

"I'm not going to let it keep me from my home." Tess walked back into the house to get her bag then returned to the deck in no time. "Take me home, Johnny."

"I don't want to scare you, but I've been a cop long enough to know when someone's lying. I don't think Emily Harris was telling me the truth about that guy. I think she's shacking up with him as we speak."

"Then I guess I have nothing to worry about."

Her fear began to subside, and she longed for her life to be normal again. Yet the hurt still remained. She hadn't been able to break down his walls.

"I still don't like the idea of taking you home."

"Being here has only put more pressure on you. I could tell that much by the way you attacked that poor kid."

"I admit, I could've handled that differently, but I'd hardly call it an attack."

"What would you call what went on between us in the bathroom before the doorbell rang?"

She couldn't let him go, couldn't leave this house without giving Johnny the chance to open up, to tell her what she had waited so long to hear.

"I'm no good to anyone right now." He went to her, everything from his facial expression to the tone in his voice reminding Tess of another moment from long ago, the first time Johnny had let her down. "I'm sorry, Tess. I can't give you what you want. I'll only end up pulling you down with me."

"Then we have nothing left to say." It took everything in her not to lose it and feel like a heartbroken teenager all over again. "I hope you find what you're looking for."

"It's not that simple."

"It is if you want it to be. I'm calling a cab."

Tess left him leaning against the railing of the deck. She had failed, truly thought their love, a love that obviously wasn't there, could bring Johnny out of his shell, back to the living, back into her life.

She waited for the cab at the end of his driveway. Once it arrived, Tess hopped in and never looked back. Giving the situation a final slap of reality, Johnny didn't stop her.

During the drive home Tess thought of all the happiness that could've come from their resurfaced friendship, from their night of passion. None of it mattered now. Johnny's scars were too deep, and Tess couldn't heal them.

He needed to do it all on his own.

As the cab rounded the corner of her street, Tess dug through her purse for some cash, instructing the driver that her house was the fourth driveway on the left. She stepped out, told him to keep the change and headed up the front steps.

Her mailbox was heaping from the morning delivery. Glad to be home, and taking in the fresh air, Tess sorted the mail on the porch. It consisted mostly of magazines and junk mail, a few bills here and there, but there was one envelope that stood out from the rest.

Tess found herself looking up and down the street, to each side of her house, to the courtyard in the center of the cul-de-sac... There was no dark-colored SUV in sight. She slipped her finger under the flap of the sealed pink envelope, stirring up a flowery scent. Tess slowly removed the matching pink card, startled by the picture imprinted upon it.

Six lavender tulips.

Tess dropped the card. The envelope floated along with it.

Under normal circumstances, Tess would have taken the card for an invitation to any number of events, a shower or a home-interior party. It could've been a thank-you note for that matter. However, seeing the tulips, the same flowers that Tess had left at Lindsey's gravesite, hit too close to home. Again, Tess surveyed her surroundings. There was nothing out of the ordinary, other than her sitting on her porch, the blood drained from her face in a panic, staring at the fallen card. Oh, how she wished Johnny could have been there with her now, but he wasn't. He had pushed Tess away, and she had pushed right back.

She was alone with no other choice but to pick up the card and read the message inside. Tess slowly opened the sweet-scented card.

If you continue on this path, he'll only end up killing you, too.

Tess turned it over, her hand shaking. There was no signature, nothing more to be read. She wasn't surprised to see that the envelope didn't have a return address, but she became alarmed after realizing it didn't contain a postal seal either. The envelope had been dropped in her mailbox.

Whoever sent this message had been at her doorstep.

Tess no longer felt safe in her home. What if they were in her house? Hiding in her garage? She rummaged through her bag in search of her cell phone, cursing herself for having parked the car inside.

When Tess turned on the phone, an envelope appeared on its screen. She hadn't checked the phone since leaving for dinner with Johnny the evening before, but now wasn't the time to worry about her messages.

With no one to turn to, she found herself dialing

147

information with an urgent need to get hold of Johnny. She should've known his number would be unlisted. He was a detective for God's sake. As an alternative, Tess dialed the police department and the receptionist put her through to Johnny's office. Had he gone back to work?

"Dawson Valley P.D."

"Johnny?" Tess blurted out.

"No, this is Detective Foster. Can I help you?"

Great, Tess thought. This was not what she needed right now.

"Mike, it's Tess. Is Johnny there?" She wasn't looking for a conflict.

"Well, well... What can I do for you today?" he responded with typical cockiness.

"I just left Johnny at his house. Did he come back to the station?"

"Nope." Mike expressed amusement at his lack of help. "But after seeing him earlier, taking the brunt of his attitude, it seems you've brought out the best in him yet again."

"I don't have time for this. Please, give me his number."

"You know the drill, Tess. For me to give out his information would be going against company policy."

"Damn it, Mike, please, this is an emergency!"

"Sorry, no can do."

Mike Foster hadn't been sorry a day in his life.

"Tess."

His voice caught her off guard. She had been so involved in trying to get Johnny's number from the arrogant bastard on the other end of her line that she hadn't realized Johnny was there, parked at the curb, sitting in his vehicle.

Tess quickly turned away from Johnny and whispered into her phone, "Go to hell, Mike." She ended the call and ran to Johnny. "Thank God you're here."

"Look, Tess..." He stepped out of the SUV. "I don't want to leave things like this between us."

"Don't worry about that now." She fumbled with the card. "This was in my mailbox." Johnny quickly snatched the card from her hand. "I just called the station, but Mike wouldn't give me your number. I didn't know who to turn to."

"Are you okay?" Johnny climbed in the backseat of his vehicle, reaching for a plastic bag. "I doubt we'll find any other prints on this, but I'm going to have it analyzed." He locked the bag in the glove compartment. "Have you been inside?"

"No, I was too afraid." Though the air was humid, Tess found herself rubbing the chill from her arms.

"You did the right thing." Johnny removed his handgun from its holster. "Give me your keys."

"What're you doing?"

"I want you to get in there and lock the doors." Johnny led Tess inside the SUV, penetrating her with a hard glare. "I'm serious, Tess, stay put!"

She nodded, handing over her house key, unable to stop from reaching out and grabbing Johnny's arm. "Please, be careful."

Johnny leaned in, lightly placing a kiss on her lips. "I'll be fine. Promise me you won't move."

"I promise."

Johnny closed the door. His kiss still warm on her lips, Tess watched as he entered the house, his gun drawn, her fear for his safety overshadowing her own. If she lost him now she would be left with so many regrets.

CB

Inside, the house was dark, the curtains shut, doors closed. Johnny entered the living room with caution, flipping on each light switch as he made his way toward the kitchen, aiming the gun in the direction of the dining room as he passed.

If the son of a bitch was in Tess's house, Johnny was going to find him.

It hadn't taken long after she had left his house for him to realize he needed her. He had been a fool for far too long, and a life without Tess wasn't something he was willing to give up on. He had pushed her away, repeatedly, but now he was ready to fight for her.

For the both of them.

There were no signs of an intruder in the downstairs of the house. Everything appeared untouched. That wasn't to say someone wasn't hiding upstairs. Before heading up, he took a look in the garage, in Tess's car, but found that area to be clean, too.

Making his way to the open staircase, Johnny stopped at the front window. Tess was still in his SUV. His gaze went to the first step. He approached, halted before proceeding up. He listened. The faint sound of a lullaby grazed his ears.

Johnny climbed the stairs, two by two, doing his best to remain undetected. Reaching the top, his manner switched from wanting to kill the person who was stalking Tess, wanting to rip him from limb to limb, back to being a cop, preparing for a run-in with the intruder.

His hold tightened around the nine-millimeter handgun, the safety off. The weapon was drawn, and he was ready to react to the worst.

The light at the end of the narrow hallway drew Johnny in its direction, the music more apparent. It was Tess's bedroom, the only bedroom besides the loft which he'd entered. The door was half-closed. It was important that he handle the situation correctly. One false move and everything could go wrong in a flash.

Two inches from the door, with one swift kick, Johnny broke into the room. "Police!"

It was empty.

His gaze immediately fell upon the music box placed in the center of Tess's bed, the pink envelope resting against its front. It took everything in him to turn away from the display in order to inspect the closet, the master bath. The house was completely empty. Johnny quickly went to the window to check on Tess.

She was safe.

Johnny walked to the bed and fell to his knees in shock. It wasn't the first time he had seen that music box. It had been Lindsey's, a gift from her parents when she had been a baby. It hadn't been long since he'd last touched it, heard its tune. Whoever had been in Tess's house had invaded Johnny's, too.

Johnny had tried giving the music box to Lindsey's parents, but they had insisted that he keep it. He had placed it in a container and put it in the attic of the farmhouse. Its lullaby had reminded Johnny of Lindsey's lies, of the baby she had never told him about, of the mysterious letters he had found written before her death.

No longer caring about adding fingerprints to the evidence, wanting to get back to Tess, Johnny grabbed the envelope and ran down the stairs. The instant he came though the front door, Tess shot out of the vehicle.

"What is it? What did you find?"

Johnny didn't respond. He tore open the pink envelope and pulled out the card, identical to the one Tess had found in her mailbox. He looked at Tess, the fear in her eyes unmistakable, his adrenaline pumping at a dangerous rate. Johnny read the card in silence...

Detective Sawyer... We meet again. You'll be sorry for what you've done... You'll both be sorry.

Whoever the sick son of a bitch was... he wasn't after Tess. He wanted Johnny. The question was, why was he using Johnny's dead wife as his pawn?

Chapter Eleven

"What does it say?" Tess felt violated. Someone had been in her house. "Damn it, Johnny, what's the note say?"

"When that woman called you..." Johnny went to his SUV and opened the glove box. "Tell me again what she said to you."

Tess would never forget the eeriness in the woman's voice, never forget those three words for as long as she lived.

"'You'll be sorry.'" Thinking back on it gave her cold chills. Johnny held the card up for her to read. "Oh, my, God."

"I found this on your bed, along with a music box."

"I don't have a music box."

"It's not yours." He put the envelope in the plastic bag along with the note Tess had received.

"You're beginning to scare me. Whose music box is it? Why is someone doing this to me?"

Uncontrollable sobs escaped her.

She had always considered herself to be a strong woman, but there was only so much she could take. Johnny wrapped his arm around her shoulder, comforting her as he unclipped the cell phone from his belt. She laid her head against him, his hand stroking the side of her face.

"This is Detective Sawyer. I need a black-and-white at 233 Holly Ridge Drive," he instructed the station. "Tell forensics I want the whole place dusted for prints." He hit the end button and dialed again. "Are you working on anything?" Johnny paused. "Good, I need you over at Tess's. Now." He hung up.

"Are you going to tell me what's going on?" Johnny was holding something back. "What aren't you telling me?"

"It's about time we play this by the book. Come on. Let's go inside. Mike and the others will be here soon." He took her hand as they walked to the house. "Don't touch anything."

Once inside, Johnny led Tess up to her room. There was so much she wanted to ask, yet words didn't come easy. There she was, in her own home, petrified of what was waiting for her around every corner. With each step, her heart skipped a beat.

They reached her bedroom doorway, Johnny stepping through the threshold first. Tess followed. There it was, the strange music box centered on her bed.

"I don't have a lot of time to get into this with you right now, but I promise... After I fill Mike and the forensics team in on what's been going on, I'll tell you everything."

"Why were you so sure the music box wasn't mine?" Tess couldn't pull her gaze away from the white box, painted with pink ribbons, a picture of a smiling baby displayed on its front.

"Because it was Lindsey's."

The ringing of the doorbell sounded from below.

"Johnny, how can this be—"

He held up a hand in midair to quiet her. "I promise, after the department finishes here, I'll tell you everything you need to know." He took her by the arm as they left the room. "For now, I want you to call your parents and have them come and get you."

"No." Tess froze, causing Johnny to release her arm from his hold. "I am not getting them involved."

"You can't stay here. You'll be in the way. The other officers and I are going to search this house from head to toe."

"I'll stay outside—sit in my car if I have to—but there's no way I'm going over there." Tess shook her head. "You of all people know how hard it is for me to go to my parents for help."

"I take it you and your mother haven't reconciled?"

"I tolerate her for my dad's sake. It doesn't matter, I'm not letting that bastard run me out of my home!"

"All right. Just stay out of the way but always where I can keep an eye on you."

The ruckus downstairs made them aware that Mike and the other cops had let themselves in. Tess and Johnny met them in the living room. Johnny entered into their circle. Tess stood back, listening as he gave them the details of what had been going on, watching as they went to work.

Tess couldn't help noticing the quiet argument ensuing between Johnny and Mike. Johnny was giving him hell, and for the first time, Tess thought she saw a glint of remorse on Mike's face.

Getting back to their duties, setting aside whatever personal problems they had, both men slipped their hands into latex gloves and set out on scouring Tess's house for clues. As they walked past, Johnny hit Tess with an unspoken warning to stay in sight, and, surprisingly, Mike stopped.

"I'm sorry for being an asshole when you called." She could tell it wasn't easy for him to apologize. "Don't worry, we're going to get this guy."

"I appreciate your help," Tess said.

Mike nodded, then joined in the search.

Tess sat in the chaise longue, looking around her house. The place had always brought her such joy, had given her comfort, a sense of safety. After everything that had taken place in the last two days, a stranger entering her house, she didn't think she'd ever feel safe alone in the house again.

Closing her eyes, Tess leaned into the chair, her mind spiraling back to her bedroom, to the music box. Lindsey's music box. None of it made sense—the phone call, the man outside her door, the weird notes, threatening to make Tess and Johnny pay, insinuating that *he* would kill her, too.

Who was *he?*

Johnny?

No. Johnny would never kill anyone, let alone Tess. The thought was absurd. Still, no matter how hard she racked her brain, Tess couldn't pinpoint a single person who would put her through such turmoil.

Tess felt herself slipping, her mind spinning out of control, her head throbbing from the unnerving mystery of it all. She pulled her knees to her chest, willing her body to relax. The warmth in Johnny's eyes, his smile, comforted her as he walked past, making her feel as though nothing—no one—could get close enough to hurt her again.

Tess fell into a deep, exhausted sleep.

When she awoke, Tess was alone. There were no longer cops scurrying through her house, dusting with white powder with hopes of locating suspicious fingerprints. She sat up. The room was pitch black, save for the beam of moonlight pouring through the side window, illuminating the silhouette on her couch.

"Johnny!" Tess screamed then jumped over the back of the chaise longue and ran for the door.

"Tess, I'm right here."

A light came on. Johnny was at her side.

"How long is this going to go on?" She looked around the room. "I'm a bundle of nerves. I don't feel safe in my own home."

Johnny took her in his arms, held her close. Tess accepted his strength, held on for dear life. It was the only time she felt safe, but how long would that last? She couldn't depend on Johnny forever.

"You trust me, don't you?" he whispered.

"Yes." Her answer came easy, without giving any thought to the past, to the ramifications of Johnny hurting her again in the future.

Somehow Tess knew he would never betray her again, but would he be enough to keep her safe?

"I want you to look me in the eye." Johnny inched back, lifting her chin with his forefinger, tracing her lower lip with his thumb. "I'm not going to let anyone hurt you. I'm going to catch this guy, and when I do, he'll pay for putting you through this."

Johnny brought his lips to hers, kissing her slowly, thoroughly, forcing all the past betrayals, regrets and present doubts to evaporate from her mind. All these years, Tess had craved such closeness, to be held in a man's protective embrace, to feel loved again by Johnny Sawyer.

In that moment, all of Tess's dreams came alive.

After the kiss ended, Tess became lost in her own private thoughts, and the nightmare threatening her happiness rushed back tenfold.

"Did you find anything?"

"Not a single print." Johnny took out his cell. "What do you say we order dinner? I believe I owe you a pizza." He nudged her, trying to bring out a smile. "After we eat, we'll sit down and get this all out on the table. I know you have a lot of questions—about a lot of things—and I promised you I would answer them."

"Will you?" Tess nestled her face against his neck. "Will you tell me everything?"

"Everything."

After the pizza arrived, Johnny did a surveillance of the house, checking windows, doors, making sure the outside motion lights were activated before joining Tess on the couch, the pizza box open on the coffee table before them. They ate in silence. The tension in the air was thick. Tess was apprehensive about what he would reveal during the long-overdue heart-to-heart.

There was no going back now.

"Where do we start?" Tess asked, breaking the ice, hoping Johnny wouldn't withdraw back into his shell.

"Why don't I tell you why I came back here after you left my place?" Tess nodded and Johnny continued. "Ever since Lindsey died, I've been an emotional wreck. I've blamed myself for her death, and I still do."

"But it wasn't your—"

"Let me finish... After you and I made love, I began to wonder if I had ever given my marriage a chance."

"I don't understand. You must've loved Lindsey or you wouldn't have married her."

A shadow of failure appeared in his eyes. "I did love her. Hell, we were married for over nine years. But what I felt last night, here with you, opened my eyes to something that I thought I'd buried deep inside years ago." Johnny took Tess's hands in his, kissed each palm. "I've never stopped loving you."

His confession reached her heart the instant the words left his lips. Though she felt totally filled with love, she couldn't hold back the feelings of regret for having lost so many years with Johnny.

There's no going back, Tess reminded herself. But it was now possible to move forward. And brave forward she did. "There hasn't been one day that has gone by that I haven't loved you."

"I never wanted to push you away, but I've been such a mess. I didn't want to hurt you again." He ran the back of his hand along her face. "I want you to know that being here now, last night, has nothing to do with Lindsey's death or my emotional state." Johnny's gaze followed the hand tracing her cheek. His eyes met hers. "It's always been you, Tess. Always."

"You can't imagine what it means to hear you say that." Tess leaned in, softly kissing the corner of his mouth, his lower lip. "But Johnny, you need to make peace with what has happened this last year, or we don't have a chance."

What if her assessment ended their conversation and pulled Johnny back into that dark hole of guilt with no chance of opening up to her again?

"You're right." Johnny got up and went to the window, his back to Tess, his reflection visible against the glass. "Without getting into all the gory details, Lindsey and I had a rocky marriage. The last two years were the worst. The night she died, she called me at the station, we fought, she accused me of never being there for her..." Johnny turned back to Tess. "She had become so unbearable. She had definitely been going through something, but I never had the chance to find out what. She hung up on me the night she died and left me with a bunch of unanswered questions."

"I am so sorry." Tess went to him.

"Don't be. You have no idea the things I've turned up since her death."

"What do you mean?" Tess asked, not wanting him to stop.

"I found a pregnancy test. It was positive."

"You didn't know?"

"Nope, she never bothered to tell me. Then there were the letters... Lindsey had been writing back and forth with someone, but she never addressed the letters I found, ones she had yet to mail. Whoever had been writing back to her knew about our entire life, our marriage, our problems, everything."

"Do you think she was having an affair?" Tess braved the question.

He shrugged. "There's no way to be sure. There weren't any envelopes with the letters. No name, no address. But from reading their correspondences, I got the impression a man had been on the receiving end."

"That is strange."

"Tess, I'm almost certain that the man who Lindsey had been writing to and your stalker are one and the same."

"What would he want with me?" Tess couldn't believe her ears. "How do I fit into this puzzle?"

"The letter you found, and the one I found in your room, they were written on the same cards as the ones I found addressed to Lindsey."

"Lavender tulips... They were her favorite."

"The music box. Someone broke into my house in order to plant it here. Somehow they knew I'd find it because that card was addressed to me. And that lullaby..." He shook his head. "The music box had been wound up, the music playing, when I found it on your bed. It was as though they wanted the music to haunt me. As if they knew—"

"That Lindsey had been pregnant."

All the pieces were coming together.

"Yes." He went back to the couch, pinching the bridge of his nose as if fighting off the comings of a headache. "It's not you who this person wants. It's me, and he's using you and Lindsey as pawns in his sick game."

"It would make sense that this person is a man, but none of this explains the phone call I got."

"I've been thinking about that." He ran his hands through his hair, massaging his temples along the way. "The voice you heard could very well have been Lindsey's."

"That's impossible."

The chills were back.

"Not if it had been a recording. Who's to say Lindsey and this mystery man hadn't talked on the phone?"

"You're the detective." She sighed. "What about Emily Harris and what her sister said about the guy she was having an affair with? The SUV?"

"I don't know, a coincidence, maybe. Seeing as I talked to Emily, it's not really relevant to this. She denied the affair."

"This whole thing is crazy," Tess said.

"Yeah, but it's not going away." Johnny pulled her close. "And neither am I. Until we find this guy, I'm staying right here. I'll never let you down again."

"I believe you."

"Are you going to be okay staying here, knowing that man was here, in your room?" He held her close.

"That's another thing. If the music box was playing when you went up there..." Tess's gaze slowly ran the length of the stairs, from bottom, to top, across the loft, to the vicinity of her room. "He must have been here minutes before you arrived, watching me on the porch, knowing that you'd come." She nestled farther into his embrace.

"I know, but don't worry." He pulled back, gazing down

161

with determination. "I'm not going to let anything happen to you."

"I'm counting on it. How do you think he got in?"

"We don't know for sure. There were no apparent signs of entry. If one of the locks had been picked, there weren't any scratches to pinpoint it. Your alarm hadn't been set."

"I'll never make that mistake again. Thank God you're here."

"I'm not going anywhere." Johnny released her. "Are you ready to go up to bed?"

"Yes," Tess lied, not wanting Johnny to know how scared she really was.

"First I want to make sure that alarm's set."

They went to the control pad by the front door. Tess pushed the button. Although she had set the device time and time again, she looked to Johnny for reassurance.

"Good." Johnny held out his hand. "Ready?"

"Ready."

This time when they entered her room, Tess knew what to expect, yet the feelings overtaking her were stronger than she had anticipated. She felt violated, but most of all, she had never felt more vulnerable, knowing that a stranger had entered her home and was still out on the streets, running free.

"If this is too much, we can go back to my house," Johnny suggested.

"Is your house any safer?" It was more of a statement than a question.

"I had Mike and two other cops go over and sweep the place for clues. They're probably still there, but—"

"No. I am not going to let this bastard chase me out of my home." Tess went to her closet and pulled out a silk robe. "I'm going to take a shower."

"Go ahead. I have to make some calls, but I'll be right here."

She went to him.

"Please... Come with me."

For the longest time Tess stood there, holding his hand in hers, their gazes locked. Though Johnny was there, in her bedroom, she wanted him closer, wanted him to make her forgot, to feel his reassuring touch.

He wasn't responding.

Maybe she had been too forward. But after everything that had developed between them in such a short time, she didn't regret it. There was still someone out there with vengeance in his blood, and Tess wasn't about to take one more second of her life for granted.

She let go of Johnny's hand, his eyes still heavy with hesitation, and continued on to the bathroom. Alone. She opened the sliding glass door and turned the water as hot as it would go. Steam rushed into the room as she stripped off her clothes.

Stepping in, taking one last look at the empty doorway, Tess closed the glass panel behind her and adjusted the water, keeping it as hot as her body would allow, desperately wanting to wash away all the fear.

Just then, the lights dimmed. Tess stiffened but didn't panic. As the shadow approached the glass, she felt her stomach lurch, felt it stir with desire. She put her hand to the gold knob, slowly opening the smoked glass door to meet his gaze.

Johnny stood there, as naked as she, the same hunger in his eyes. Tess extended her hand, wanting nothing more than to have the hot water plastering her body, to feel Johnny's touch burning her senses.

Neither of them said a word. He joined her in the shower, shutting the door to the rest of the world. With utmost gentleness, he moved in close, raising both her arms over her head, his mouth fixed on hers, with the warmth of the ceramic tile against her back. Once again, Johnny made Tess feel safe, loved. And no one—not even the stalker—could take that sense of security away from her.

∽

That night, Johnny didn't leave Tess's side. He stayed awake, watching her sleep, listening to her breathe. They couldn't go on like this. He knew it and deep down so did she.

Whoever was after Johnny wasn't going to rest until he got what he wanted, but there was no way Johnny was going to let him hurt Tess in the process. He needed to convince her to get out of the house, to go somewhere safe, until he could put this guy away for good.

But Johnny knew better than anyone that Tess was not going to be an easy sell. She was the most stubborn woman he knew. If he had his way, he'd bring her to the station and lock her up safely in a cell until the whole mess was over.

He slipped out of bed and went to the window seat. *What a weekend.* If someone had told him last Friday that by Sunday his life would be altered drastically, he would have laughed in their face. He had lost hope of ever finding happiness again.

However, seeing Tess in the parking lot after work that day with Rex Cramer coming on to her, something in him had snapped back into place. Throughout the last thirty hours his mind had been pulled in a zillion different directions, but he had known, right then and there, that he wanted Tess back in his life.

His gaze went to the bed. Tess was mumbling, stirring in her sleep, the effects of the break-in, the letters, still heavy on her mind. Seeing what this was doing to her, Johnny's fury began to erupt from within.

He needed to find the man behind all the madness.

The light on Johnny cell phone flickered as it vibrated atop the nightstand. He shot up, grabbed the phone and disappeared into the adjoining bathroom. He looked at the caller I.D. *Restricted.*

Johnny clenched his fist, holding the phone in the other hand. His cell was a private line with a private number. He never received restricted calls. This had to be...

"Yeah," Johnny whispered, not wanting to wake Tess.

"Detective Sawyer," the faint male voice said. "I see you got my message."

"Listen, you son of a bitch, if you ever come near Tess again—"

"Oh, Tess, what a beauty she's become."

The man's voice... Johnny knew that voice.

"It's me you want. Why don't you face me like a man?" Johnny needed to keep him talking, needed to place that distant voice.

"After what you've done, Sawyer, that's rich of you to say." His tone turned violent. "Better keep her close... It would serve you right if something happened to that beautiful bitch of yours."

"I'll kill you." The words rolled past Johnny's lips. "If you lay one finger on Tess, I will kill you."

"Thanks for the pizza."

Click.

"What the hell..." Johnny dropped his cell and ran down the stairs.

The coffee table had been cleared of the pizza, replaced with an instant photo of Tess and Johnny behind the steamed glass of her shower.

Chapter Twelve

"Morning."

"Mike?" Tess sat up, looking around her bedroom. "What're you doing here? Where's Johnny?"

"Just calm down, everything's going to be okay."

"You didn't answer my question." Tess flung her legs over the edge of the bed, the sheet wrapped tightly around her. "Do you mind?"

"As a matter of fact, I do. I'm not letting you out of my sight."

Mike's sarcasm drove Tess crazy.

"Then go stand over there and turn your head." She waited until Mike reached the other end of the room before ripping the sheet from the bed and hurrying to the bathroom for her robe. "Thank you."

"Don't mention it." Mike pulled out a pack of cigarettes. "Do you mind?"

"No, not if you'll tell me what's going on here. Where's Johnny?"

"Just sit down and wait." He lit the cigarette and inhaled deep, staring out the window.

"Damn it, I've had about enough of this crap!" Tess headed to the doorway, but Mike grabbed her arm. "Get your hands off of me."

"You can't go downstairs."

"Why the hell not?"

"Because they're investigating a crime scene."

Tess went numb.

"Oh my God... Johnny!" She ripped her arm from Mike's grasp and ran for the door, but he effortlessly pulled her back into the room, slamming the door shut. "He's down there, isn't he? That man came back and hurt Johnny, didn't he!"

Without warning, the door flew open and Johnny appeared in the bedroom, safe and sound. Alive. Tess threw herself in his arms, her eyes pinched shut, holding back tears, an unbelievable sense of relief washing over her.

"I'm right here," Johnny said, his lips upon her forehead.

"When Mike told me I couldn't go downstairs, I thought..." Tess opened her eyes, cradled her hand to the side of his face. "I thought I'd lost you."

"That's not going to happen." Johnny put an arm around her shoulder, walking her farther into the room, her back facing the door. "We're both going to make it through this, but I need your help."

"Anything. I'll do anything if it'll help put a stop to this man." She nodded toward the door, wondering how she could have slept through the obvious chaos going on downstairs. "Johnny, what happened?"

"He was here."

"How could that be? You checked everything—twice. How could he have gotten in?"

"I don't know."

"Why is he doing this to me?" She was in tears. "What does he want?"

"It's me he wants. Not you," Johnny said.

The stress had finally taken its toll. It felt as though her mind was spiraling out of control with visions of Johnny tangled up with stalkers, guns, strangers invading her home. She sat on the disheveled bed, burying her face in her hands. "When is this going to end?"

"Right now." The voice came from the hallway.

Tess looked up.

"Dad?"

"Sweetheart, thank God you're okay." Eric Fenmore dropped to his knees and held his daughter. "Johnny filled me in on all that's been going on."

Tess met Johnny's gaze. The pit in her stomach grew. He knew she didn't want her family involved. Yet he had gone ahead and contacted her father, anyway. It could only mean one thing.

Johnny wanted her out of the way, wanted to face this mess on his own.

"No, don't even think about it." She eased out of her father's hold and went to Johnny. "What aren't you telling me? Why'd you call my dad?"

"Can you give us a minute?" Johnny nodded to both Mike and Eric Fenmore.

"I'll be right outside." Her dad gently squeezed her arm. "Listen to him, Tess."

She waited for the room to clear. Her dad went first and Mike followed, briefly stopping as Johnny whispered something in his ear. Mike responded with a nod. Johnny closed the door.

The desperation in his eyes was too much to bear. He was

pulling away again. She knew what was coming. She didn't want to have this discussion, but it was inevitable.

"Tess, this has gotten out of control." He stood by the door, made no attempt to come to her. "This guy's out for blood, and I'm afraid of what he'll do the next time he manages to get this close to you."

"There won't be a next time." She shook her head frantically, rambling on, "We'll be more careful. You can put one of your officers at the door. I won't leave the house. Johnny, we can't let this freak control our lives like this!"

Tess held back a sob, went to Johnny, tried taking him in her arms, pleading for him to listen, but he held her back by her shoulders.

"Stop!"

"But what if—"

"Tess, stop." His voice had softened, his grip relaxed. "I'm a cop. This is what I do. It's my job to keep you safe."

"What happened last night?" Tess still wasn't quite sure.

"It doesn't matter. All you need to know is that bastard got way too close. It's not going to happen again. This time..." He released her, went to the window. "This time I'm going after him."

"Maybe there's a way I can help. He initially contacted me, remember?" She loved him so much and would do anything for him, even risk her life for his.

"That's exactly why you're going home with your dad. You'll be safe there."

"That's what you said when you brought me to your house." Tess was not giving in to Johnny without a fight. "How can you be sure that he won't find me there, too? How do you know he's not watching this house now? He probably already knows my dad's here."

"Let us do our job. I can't let my feelings get in the way of doing the right thing." Johnny started for the door. "It's an order, Tess. I'm telling you, as a cop, that you're leaving this house right now. You're going to do exactly what I and the rest of the department tell you."

"Damn you!" The anger was back. Once again, the past, the hurt, the present dangers, his attitude, it was all building up inside her. Once again, she was being treated like a child, given no choice in the matter.

"Look..." Johnny turned to her. "This is for your own good. I can't keep you safe. I'm too close to you. I can't do my job when I'm worried about you. Why can't you understand that I'm doing this because I love you!" Reluctantly, Tess backed off, realized she was being treated like a child because she was acting like one. "Do you hear me—I love you."

Tess fell into his arms, held him tight. She was scared for him, scared she would never have the chance to be this close to him again. Scared that after everything was over, he wouldn't be there to come back to her.

"Promise me you'll be careful, promise me you'll call the minute you catch this guy."

"You know I will."

"Are you taking me to my parents' house?"

"No. You're going to go with Mike and do everything he says. It's all set."

"Are you staying here?" He didn't answer, only shook his head from side to side. "Where will you be?"

"I need to leave." He pulled back. "I don't want you worrying about me. As long as you do as you're told, everything's going to be all right."

Johnny leaned in, kissing each corner of her mouth. Tess closed her eyes, savoring his touch, searing the feeling into her mind as if it were the last time she would feel his lips on hers.

No.

She wouldn't accept that. She had no choice but to trust Johnny, trust that he would come back to her, trust in his love for her because she loved him more than anything in the world.

"I've never stopped loving you, Johnny. Now that we've found each other again... I don't know what I'd do if I lost you."

"You're not going to lose me." He opened the bedroom door and peered out into the hallway. "We're ready." He went to the chair by the closet. "Here, it's the bag you brought to my house. Do you think this'll be enough for a couple of days?"

"A couple of days? What about my job?"

"I've already talked to your boss." Johnny lifted a hand to quiet her. "Before you ask, yes, this is necessary."

"I trust you." She had to.

"Remember what I said."

He hugged her close. Tess could feel the uncertainty in his strong arms. He was hesitant to let her go. Johnny was scared, too.

"Please, be careful." She fought to hold back the tears. "I love you, Johnny."

"I love you, too," Johnny whispered against her ear. "More than you know."

Then he was gone.

◌ঌ

"Where's my father?" Tess asked Mike.

"He's waiting for you at his house." Mike lifted the sleeve of his suit coat. "Damn, where the hell is she?"

"Who?"

"Tess number two." He smirked. "Like the world needs another one of you."

"What're you talking about?" Though Mike had apologized the night before, Tess had been wrong to think they could ever be friends.

His cell phone rang.

"Tell me you're on your way." Mike waited, listened. "You've got to be kidding me. No, no, don't call him. I'll handle it." He pressed the end button. "Johnny won't like this."

"Tell me what's going on," Tess said. "What isn't Johnny going to like?"

"It's time for you to go." Mike put his arm through Tess's and started for the door. "Your parents are waiting."

"You know what's going on, don't you? This plan of Johnny's?"

"Of course I do, we're partners."

Tess stopped and plopped herself down on the bedroom floor.

"What the hell are you doing?" Mike stared in shock. "Get up."

"I'm not moving until you tell me what that phone call was about."

"The hell you're not. Get up." Mike reached down and pulled Tess's arm. "We don't have time for your games."

"Who was on the phone?" Mike rolled his eyes at her, and Tess felt as though she was close to getting him to let her in on their plan. "I mean it, Mike, you're going to have to carry me out of here if you don't—"

"All right, all right!" He raked his fingers through his bangs. "The woman on the phone was a cop. She was supposed to come here as a decoy, hopefully lure that bastard in again, so we can snag his ass. Now she's delayed, and our plan's going to go right out the window." Mike paced the floor in front of Tess. "Are you satisfied? Now come on, I don't have all day. I have to drop you off, then call Johnny."

This time Mike succeeded in pulling Tess up off the floor.

"Wait!" She broke free of his hold. "You're not going to call Johnny."

"You're way out of your league and in no position to be throwing orders around. Let's go."

"Will you just listen to me?" Tess waited until Mike stopped in the hallway. "Where's Johnny? I take it he's watching the house from somewhere nearby?"

"He will be, and he's going to be pretty pissed off if I mess this up."

"But your decoy is a no-show," Tess reminded Mike.

"That's why I need to get the hell out of here and find another cop!"

"Use me."

"You're out of your damn mind! No way. Johnny would have my ass." Mike tapped his cigarette pack against the heel of his hand.

Was he contemplating her idea?

"The house is secured, right?" Tess pushed on. "You guys must have cops everywhere. And what about all the noise I heard downstairs?" She aimed a finger past Mike. "The house is rigged up, isn't it?"

"You've watched one too many cop shows."

"I'm right, aren't I?"

"Damn it, Tess, Johnny would kill me if I left you here! Once that door's shut, everything's set in motion. The cameras, everything! There'll be no going back."

"I realize this isn't a game. My life is on the line." If Mike had a caring bone in his body, by God, Tess was going to find it. "You have to admit I have a better chance of luring this guy in than some look-alike. I know that Johnny would never agree to this, but, Mike, it's because he's too close to me."

"He would never forgive me if something happened to you."

"I'll be careful. Please, let me do this."

"There are cameras everywhere on the first floor, and no one can get in through the second. We'll see everything, be watching your every move." Mike walked down the stairs and Tess followed. "If the phone rings, you answer it. Act normal. I want to see a thumbs-up every minute to let us know you're okay." Mike held his arm at his side, made a fist and extended his thumb. "Like this, do you understand me?"

"I can do this." Tess nodded.

"For all of our sakes, I hope so." He went to the door. "We're pretty sure this guy's watching the house. The second I walk out this door, you're on. Be careful. Don't make me regret this."

Mike opened the front door, stepped over the threshold and left.

There was no going back. He was right about one thing. Johnny was not going to be happy to find out that the woman he loved had been left inside the house, being used as bait to catch a stalker.

Chapter Thirteen

"Is everything set?" Johnny asked after Mike entered the attic of the house situated diagonal from Tess's.

"Fire it up."

Johnny went through the digital board, flipping on interior and exterior cameras. It hadn't been difficult getting Tess's neighbors to let the Dawson Valley P.D. use their attic as a makeshift stakeout site. Tess was very well liked, and the idea of a stranger roaming their quiet street had left them more than willing to help out.

"It's all functioning." Johnny looked at each screen, stopping, zooming when he reached the living room. "I hope this works."

"We'll catch him." Mike adjusted the cameras surrounding Tess's property.

"Make sure we have a clear view of the street from both directions."

"Got it."

"How was Tess when you left her at the Fenmores'?"

"Don't worry about her, man. She's a tough girl."

"She puts on a strong front, but I know she's scared as hell." Johnny checked his watch, his cell phone, then swiveled in the chair. "I hope you were decent to her."

"We have action," Mike blurted out.

Johnny's body tensed. His eyes shot from screen to screen, then to Mike. "It's a damn dog."

"Can't be too sure."

"By the way, nice touch," Johnny said.

"Huh?"

"The deputy, she's wearing Tess's clothes." Johnny clicked the button, zooming in for a clearer view. "Did you shut the sound off on the interior cameras?"

"No, why?"

"Cause the second I zoomed in, she gave the thumbs-up at her side." Johnny's eyes traveled over the screens.

"I told her to do it continuously."

"Hope she doesn't plan on standing there all day. I can't see through that window." Johnny tried moving the camera to the right. "What the hell?"

"What's up?" Mike leaned over Johnny's shoulder.

"Come on, turn, turn, that's it, a little more. Damn it!" Johnny jumped up from the chair, pinning Mike to the wall in no time flat. "That's Tess!"

"The deputy called, said she couldn't make it in time." Mike shoved Johnny back. "You know Tess... That woman's got a thick skull, threw herself on the floor and wouldn't leave!"

"I cannot believe you left her in there." Johnny sat in front of the screen, staring at Tess, compiling in his mind all the things he was going to say when he saw her. "I'm getting her out of there."

"If you go over there now, you'll blow the plan to hell."

Although he didn't like it, Johnny knew Mike was right.

"You better hope we get through this with no problems."

Johnny turned to Mike. "If anything happens to her, I'm holding you responsible."

"She'll do fine. I briefed her on all the rules, told her we'd be watching her at all times. If it'll make you feel better, I can get her on the line."

"No, it'll distract her, and frankly, I'm in no mood to talk to her right now." Johnny fixed his gaze on screen two. "I might end up saying something I'll regret."

Johnny wasn't the religious type, yet he found himself saying a silent prayer, asking God to please spare Tess, to not take another woman from him. He glared at Mike, shaking his head, wanting to tear him apart for putting Tess in danger.

He couldn't put all the blame on his partner. When Tess had her mind made up, there was no stopping her. Nevertheless, Tess had gone behind his back and put her safety on the line after he had pleaded with her to stay out of it.

Now isn't the time to be pissed. He watched Tess, waited for any type of movement, once again calling upon a higher power for extra comfort.

"Make sure that window's open and the safety ladder's in place." Johnny removed his gun, then wrestled out of the shoulder holster. He placed his hand on the top of the gun, quickly pulling the slide back. With a bullet in the chamber, Johnny stuffed the gun down the back of his jeans. "We better get this son of a bitch."

അ

Tess closed the magazine she had been staring at for the last twenty minutes. She'd been afraid to walk around, afraid to look in the cameras. Was Johnny aware she'd taken the place of the designated female deputy?

He would be a force to reckon with if she made it out of the sting alive. Even so, Tess wouldn't have done things differently if given the chance. She had been too wrapped up in it to bow out.

Opening the fridge, she craved the wine resting in the door shelf but instead took out a Coke and went to the couch, giving the thumbs-up on her way. She had been trying hard to act normal, but her stomach had a mind of its own.

Tess sipped the Coke, willing the aches to subside. The waiting was killing her. She almost clicked on the television as a diversion but was afraid the noise would muffle out an intruder. Her luck, the cameras would miss it, and she would be taken away by gunpoint or shot on sight.

"Talk about the weekend from hell." Tess reached for the book on the end table.

Never in all her life had she experienced so many different emotions at once. One minute she had been making love to the man of her dreams, and in the next she'd been trying to elude a stranger, a very mysterious one at that.

The low ringing of her cell phone traveled down the stairs, the long jingle playing a happy tune. Tess made a mental note to change the ringer after she took the call.

She started up the stairs but realized Mike hadn't said anything about cameras being up there. Not wanting to scare Johnny, she quickly descended the two steps, gave a thumbs-up to the camera in the front corner of the room, then ran up after her phone.

By the time she'd dug through her bag and found it, she had missed the call. She retraced her steps to the couch, examining the screen. *Restricted.* Tess shrugged, not paying it any more attention, then remembered her voice mail. She looked at her cell and saw the little envelope flashing.

She had three voice messages.

The first was from two days before. It was her dad. The second was dead, no message, only the faint hum of breathing. Tess was concerned and almost afraid to check the last message. Just as she pressed the command to retrieve it, the phone rang.

Startled, Tess dropped it but quickly bent down and gave the camera a thumbs-up. The last thing she wanted to do was alarm Johnny. She looked at the screen. *Restricted.* It struck her. It was probably Johnny calling on a police line.

"Hello?" Tess tried remaining calm. No one answered, but she could hear someone there. *There's no going back*, she remembered—her sole purpose for being in the house was to lure this man out. "Hello? I know you're there."

She again gave a thumbs-up.

"Tess, do you remember me?" a weak female voice asked.

"Mrs. Moran?" It was Lindsey's mother.

"Yes, dear, I hope you don't mind me calling."

"Of course not."

"I ran into your dad the other day, and he gave me this number in case I couldn't reach you at home. I was wondering if we could talk?"

"Now?" Tess looked at the camera, a smile on her face, trying to comprehend the phone call.

"I'm on my way." The phone went dead.

Tess hadn't seen Lindsey's mother since the funeral. She glanced up at the camera, knowing a visit from Mrs. Moran could blow everything. But Tess wasn't in danger. Mrs. Moran had always thought a lot of Tess as a kid, as Lindsey's best friend. Johnny would see it was Lindsey's mother at the door. Maybe it would ease his mind that she wasn't alone.

Tess gave the camera another thumbs-up.

ભ

"Who the hell is she talking to?" Johnny was out of his head with worry.

"She's a smart girl. Everything's fine."

"Since when did you become part of Tess's fan club?" Johnny gave his partner a sideward glance.

"Let's just say I have a newfound respect for the woman." Mike nodded to the screen. "This takes real guts."

"It's more like pure ignorance," Johnny mumbled. "Look, there's a car." The cop in Johnny went into overdrive. He stood. The daylight made it easy for him to identify the vehicle before it reached its destination. "Wait a minute." He looked to Mike. "That's the Morans' car."

"Tess sees them, too." Mike pointed to screen number two. "Maybe that's who she was talking to. Look, Tess is letting us know she's fine."

Though Johnny saw her smile, saw her thumb extended at her side, he knew something wasn't right, knew it wouldn't be Lindsey's mother stepping out of that car.

"Oh, God, no..." Johnny watched as Tess went to the front door. "I'm out of here!" he screamed to Mike.

Johnny jumped through the attic window and scaled halfway down the portable fire ladder in a panic. The car was almost all the way up Tess's driveway. He had been right. It was Lindsey's parents' car.

He should've felt a sense of relief but none came. He went down a few more rungs. He reached for the gun in the back of his pants, watched the brake lights of the car shine red, listened as the engine shut off.

Tess appeared on her doorstep, looking toward the house where Johnny found himself situated against the outside wall, her thumb barely visible.

"She's saying she's okay," Mike yelled from the attic above.

That wasn't good enough. Johnny descended the ladder, which ended just below the second floor of the house, then jumped the rest of the way. He remained out of sight, watching, waiting for someone to step out of the car. His heart skipped a beat. What the hell was Tess doing?

She was approaching the car.

A man stepped out, a very tall man who was not Lindsey's father. Just as Johnny was ready to beat feet across the lawn, across the street to Tess's house, she went to this man, gave him a hug.

"Who the hell?" he muttered.

He should have never hesitated.

In the blink of an eye, the man spun around to face Johnny, still holding Tess, her back facing the house across the street. The son of a bitch had known Johnny was there. Johnny heard Tess scream, saw the reflection of a gun held to her side.

Then the man did something that both shocked and relieved Johnny. He threw Tess to the ground and started toward him, firing three rounds along the way, but Johnny was too fast. He shot the crazed man in the right arm, again in the leg, slowing him. Wounded, the man fell to the ground.

He could hear Tess screaming, "No, Luke, please don't! Johnny!"

Johnny felt the pain as his leg began collapsing beneath him. He'd been shot.

"You okay, man?" Mike was at his side, his gun drawn and

aimed toward the fallen criminal. Cops appeared from all over the vicinity.

"Don't let that bastard hurt Tess!"

"I've got him, Johnny," Mike yelled, running across the street.

Sirens were blaring through the neighborhood, and Johnny didn't breathe a sigh of relief until he saw the man was contained. He watched as Mike rolled him over and cuffed him hard against the ground.

He saw Tess... She was running to him. Johnny's gaze dropped. *Thank you, God.* He looked to the sky, his leg throbbing in pain.

"Johnny, are you okay?" Tess fell to his side. "Oh, my God, you're shot!"

"I'm fine. Are you all right?"

"Yes, I'm sorry." She was in tears, looking from Johnny to the man at Mike's feet. "I can't believe it. All this time it's been Luke. When Mrs. Moran called, I had no idea."

"What?" Johnny tried to move. During his moment of panic, the name hadn't registered in Johnny's head, but it did now. Luke Moran. Lindsey's twin brother, a man who had spent the majority of his life in and out of correctional facilities all over the state, the man at the end of the mysterious letters written by Johnny's dead wife, who had obviously been out for revenge, blaming Johnny for the unhappiness and death of his twin sister.

"She told you about Luke?"

"No, she asked to come over but never came... Instead it was Luke."

"That son of a bitch probably used his own mother to get to you. She would've never been a part of this." Johnny gritted his teeth and reached for his leg.

"How do you think he got in my house?" Tess asked. "The alarm was set."

"He's probably been watching your every move and obtained your security code through a high-powered set of binoculars. I didn't even know he was out of jail." Johnny used the trunk of a tree to pull himself up.

"What're you doing? The ambulance is on its way." Tess turned her head. "Look, it's coming up the street. Sit back down."

"Help me take some weight off of my leg." He accepted her shoulder and together they made their way to Luke's side, Johnny nodding at Mike, letting his partner know he was okay.

"Sawyer, I should've killed you," Luke Moran grunted through gritted teeth.

"You had your chance."

"I should've never trusted that bitch Emily. If she hadn't ratted me out, I would've killed you before you had the chance to get to me! Stupid, stupid bitch!"

Now it all made sense. He should've listened to his gut, should've forced the truth out of Emily Harris. "Not that I owe you an explanation, but Emily never ratted you out. She never even mentioned knowing you—or that she was involved with you. Although she lied to me, I'm beginning to wonder if she knew what kind of monster you are."

"Think what you want, Sawyer, but it won't change the fact that because of you my sister is dead." Luke looked at Tess. "Little by little, he'll kill you, too."

"I never laid a hand on Lindsey. We had our problems, but I loved your sister."

Johnny felt the guilt resurface, felt it reach its peak. He

glanced over at Tess, knowing how much he had hurt her by being with Lindsey. But her face didn't hold any traces of pain. She smiled. Her encouragement, her love, made all the guilt go away.

"Come on," she said. "Let's get you to the ambulance." She touched her lips to Johnny's cheek. "There's nothing more for you to deal with here."

"Wait a minute," Luke called out as they walked past. Johnny and Tess faced him. "Don't you even want to know about the baby?"

"Come on," Johnny said to Tess. "I can't do this."

"Yes, you can." Tess stood, forcing Johnny to face the demons of his past.

"When Lindsey told me she was going to pass that baby off as yours, I told her she was nuts, told her to 'fess up to the affair, so you'd realize just how far you had pushed her away. Now you have nothing. My sister's dead and so is her baby— you have nothing."

"Who was the father?" Johnny asked. "Who was my wife having an affair with?"

Sick laughter erupted from Luke. "You don't deserve to know. For the rest of your life, every time you enter the police station, I want you to think of me and of what I know, and wonder... *Which one of these pieces-of-shit cops fucked my wife?*"

Johnny's stomach lurched, the bile threatening to come up. What a lie his life had been, and no matter what Luke Moran said, it hadn't been all Johnny's fault. He could now accept that. Johnny mustered up every bit of strength he had left, eased down to the ground on all fours and looked his attacker in the eye.

"You're the one who has nothing, nothing but a jail cell

185

waiting for you on the other side of a barbed-wire fence. And every time you look at those four walls closing in on you, remember me—and that I put you there." Johnny gazed into Tess's eyes, and with her help, pulled himself back up. "I have everything to live for. I can finally let go of a past that's haunted me for far too long."

"Me, too," Tess agreed, as the paramedics materialized at her side, a stretcher for Johnny and one for the criminal at his feet.

⚃

Tess rode in the ambulance with Johnny, never once letting go of his hand. They were told the bullet had just missed Johnny's main artery. They had been lucky to get out of the ordeal alive.

"Are you feeling better?" Tess asked, watching as his eyes fluttered from the pain medication.

"I'm feeling damn good right now." Johnny smiled. "But don't think I've forgotten that you went behind my back and almost got yourself killed."

"Close your eyes, it's all behind us." She rubbed the sweat-soaked hair from his forehead, leaving a kiss in its place. "When you wake up from surgery, I'll be right by your side." Tess bent down, touching her lips to Johnny's. "I love you."

"I love you, too," he mumbled before sailing off into a drug-induced sleep.

Epilogue

Tess and Johnny stood back, looking at the farmhouse through new eyes. Never in her wildest dreams had she imagined it could look this beautiful, this absolutely breathtaking—not only the house itself but the surrounding countryside as well.

The old house held so many memories, each different for both of them. An old, run-down hideout for two teenagers in love, an escape for a man who couldn't face his past, a refuge for a woman who had been thrown back into his life...

Now they were there together, as one, a reality that neither of them had ever thought possible, filled with promise that with each passing day their safe haven would only flourish more and more.

"I finished adding my touches." Johnny squeezed Tess's hand, pulling her toward the door. "Do you want to see?"

"Do I have a choice?" She laughed.

Tess shared in his smile as Johnny led her through the house until they were standing outside the room that had been left untouched, a room where they had first found love, one that they completed together.

Johnny entered first.

Tess wrapped her mind around the beautiful vision, wanting to remember this moment forever. Her pride had nothing to do with the fact that the moldings gleamed from below and above, that the once paint-flaked walls now held elegant wallpaper or that the floors gleamed in the moonlight.

No. It was a miraculous vision all its own.

One that started to take shape the day a troubled man brought a lonely woman to his home, looking for a way to keep her safe by doing his job, a job he truly loved.

Without realizing it at the time, Tess Fenmore had brought life into Johnny's house that day along with promises of new beginnings.

"So, what do you think?" he asked.

She went to Johnny's side, took his hand. "The room wouldn't be complete without it."

He looked up from the small tent, pitched below the corner window as it had been years ago, along with the white stick candles on the windowsill. Johnny smiled. Just smiled. That was more than enough to warm her soul.

Tess took such pleasure in his natural expression, for she knew it was now backed by a clean conscience, free from guilt, no more worries about what happened in the past.

Johnny was filled with pure and total contentment, every bit the man she remembered him to be. He'd brought so much to her life back then, and she knew there was much more to be had. Johnny would bring her a lifetime of happiness, and together, this time, they would beat the odds.

"Do you know how much I love you?" Johnny asked, bringing Tess back to the here and now.

"Tell me." She could never hear it enough.

"I've loved you all my life. Even during all the years apart,

I've never stopped."

Tess laid her head on his shoulder, staring out the window. The fountain outside in the garden glistened, the water flowed freely.

"I'm so glad you brought me here. The countryside, this room, you..." Tess peered up at Johnny from under heavy eyelids. "It's all so beautiful."

"We're finally going to have that happy life together." Johnny pulled her into his arms, lifting her chin. Their gazes locked, no longer filled with pain and sorrow. "Because of you, I feel alive. You gave me my life back."

"You did it all on your own."

Just when Tess thought she couldn't be happier, the gleam in Johnny's eyes proved there was still more to come. She watched as he went to each of the large windows, pulling the drapes closed, his sexy smile lighting up the darkened room every time he glanced her way.

He went to the hutch and removed a pack of matches, then handed one to Tess and together they lit the old stick candles on the windowsill above the tent as if they were kids again, sneaking away from their homes, escaping to the freedom of the countryside.

Tess could feel the heat radiating from Johnny's hand as he took hers, felt the goose bumps on her exposed arms as he lightly ran both hands to her shoulders, her neck, until he held her face.

Johnny closed the space between them.

Butterflies fluttered throughout Tess's stomach as Johnny drew her closer. She wanted to remember every detail of their first night together in the newly remodeled room. The way the full moon lit up the black night sky, the cool air seeping through half-opened windows, the flames of the candles burning strong.

"I'll be right back."

Johnny left Tess standing there, her legs weak from his touch. When he returned, he held a vase filled with red roses in one hand, a bottle of champagne and two crystal flutes in the other, a corkscrew between his teeth.

"I wonder what the guys at the station would say if they saw you now." Tess took the roses, placed them in the center of the refinished table. "You're quite the romantic."

"I'd deny it."

She watched as Johnny opened the bottle, careful not to send the cork flying. He poured them both a full glass and raised his in the air.

"To you."

"Me?"

"For making me the happiest man on earth, for making me whole again."

He clinked her glass and brought his to his lips, almost took a sip. Tess reached out and stopped him, the champagne rocking back and forth in the flute.

"Wait a minute. My turn."

"Make it fast, Fenmore, the champagne was my idea." Johnny smiled.

"I'll keep it short." She placed a hand to her heart. "Promise." He leaned in and stole a swift kiss. "I just want to say thank you."

"For what?"

"For everything. This room, for bringing me into your home, back into your life... Thank you."

"It's all yours for the taking." Johnny fanned one hand

about the room. "What do you say?" He pointed to the tent. "For old times' sake?"

"Where are you going now?" Tess asked as he turned around to leave again.

"Don't worry about it. You go on in. I'll be back in a minute."

"If you say so."

Tess pulled back the flap of the tent. Johnny had laid down a sleeping bag, along with two pillows. Tess tied up the material of the makeshift window, enabling the candlelight to flood through the dark tent.

"All right, I'm back. Close your eyes."

"What're you up to?" Tess called out from inside.

"Why do women have to ask so many questions?"

After letting out an irritated sigh, Tess situated herself in the far corner of the tent and closed her eyes, the muscles in her legs tensing up. She could feel the tent move as he made his way in beside her.

"Okay, open your eyes."

When Tess spotted the shimmering diamond Johnny held before her, all thoughts of irritation evaporated from her mind. Tears welled up in her eyes. It was the most exquisite ring she'd ever seen, a beautifully cut pear-shaped diamond surrounded by three smaller stones on each side. It wasn't until Johnny brought his hand to her face, wiping away her tears, that she realized she was crying. For once, they were tears of joy.

"I was thinking..." Johnny's voice mesmerized her, the ring held her gaze. "We make a pretty good team. Will you marry me, Tess?"

He held the ring in the palm of his hand, as Tess gazed into his eyes. Most women dreamed of their prince charming getting down on one knee to profess his undying love through a classic, romantic marriage proposal, but not Tess. The love she saw in Johnny tonight surpassed the dramatics of any childhood fantasy.

"I don't know, Detective, what do you think?"

"I'm thinking about cuffing you if I don't get an answer. You know how impatient I can be." Johnny pulled her close, taking Tess's hands in his. "Will you be my wife?"

"Johnny…" Tess tipped her head, briefly brushing her lips against his. "I would have married you eleven years ago."

"Is that your way of saying yes?"

"Yes, yes, yes!" Tess wasn't able to contain the excitement any longer as Johnny slipped the stunning ring on her finger. "Yes, I'll marry you."

For the rest of her life, she would always remember that moment. She had always believed in Johnny, and now she had the man of her dreams by her side. Forever.

She watched as Johnny's gaze dropped to her lips, his finger trailing underneath the collar of her shirt. The way he made Tess feel when his hands touched her skin, when his mouth was on hers, was like a small slice of heaven.

Had it always been in the cards for them to find love again? Surviving the past and the obstacles that threatened their future had made them stronger, had held them together. Because of Johnny, she was able to know what it felt like to belong and to be loved completely and unconditionally.

She pulled Johnny's shirt above his head, tossing it amongst the sleeping bag and pillows. They did the same with each and every piece of clothing until they both sat naked, the flames of the candles flickering in the moonlight.

The tent, which they had once used as a hideaway to

wallow in each other's pleasures, wasn't what Johnny had in mind tonight. He led Tess outside, underneath the stars. They knelt to the ground with thoughts of pure desire enrapturing their bodies in the risk of the moment.

Savoring every sound, every touch, every emotion, they rested on the dew-moistened grass where they drifted into their own little world—a place where love had overcome lies, where secrets no longer existed.

With the ghosts from their past put to rest, it was their undying passion that brought Johnny and Tess together, making them whole again, binding them forever by a love that had never died.

About the Author

To learn more about Amy Mistretta, please visit www.AmyMistretta.com. Send an email to Amy at Amy@AmyMistretta.com or join her MySpace page at www.myspace.com/amymistretta.

She stands for everything he despises. Only, the minute they meet, she becomes everything he desires.

Reilly's Promise
© 2007 Christyne Butler

Former US Marine turned private investigator, Reilly Murdock is no stranger to high society. Thanks to his malevolent millionaire stepfather, he turned his back on that elite world years ago. But when a friend calls in a favor he's honor bound to repay, Reilly finds himself stuck as glorified babysitter to a spoiled heiress with secrets of her own.

Since her father's sudden death six months ago, Cassandra Van Winter has been trying to conceal her family's millions of dollars of debt. She can't afford to let anyone near enough to discover the charade she's maintaining. At first, the discovery of a multi-million-dollar necklace seemed like the answer to her prayers, but that was before the "accidents" started.

Now, she takes one look at the six feet of muscle her mother's hired to protect her, and curses her body for coming back to life. As the "accidents" increase and danger comes closer, Reilly gets closer too. Before long it's not just her life in danger, but her heart.

Available now in ebook and print from Samhain Publishing.

Enjoy the following excerpt from Reilly's Promise...

"Cassandra darling, why don't you have a seat?" Margaret Van Winter waved a graceful hand toward a low sofa. "And there's no such thing as an ex-Marine."

Reilly's attention darted to the older woman, dressed head to toe in white, except for a blue and red scarf around her neck. Here was another surprise. Margaret Van Winter was nothing he expected a woman of her wealth and status to be. Her smile was genuine, her handshake warm and firm when they met.

How would a lady like her know Marines hated to be called "ex"?

"What did you say, Mother?"

Margaret turned back to her daughter. "I said most men who've served in the Marine Corps prefer to call themselves 'former Marines'. They never consider themselves out of the Corps. 'Once a Marine, Always a Marine.' Isn't that right, Mr. Murdock?"

She smiled as she looked his way again, and the muscles in his neck relaxed. With her silvery hair cut short and few lines on her face, Margaret Van Winter wore her age with grace and beauty. "Yes, ma'am."

"Former Marine, ex-Marine," Cassandra said. "I don't care what he's called or what he was. I'll tell you what he isn't. He isn't my bodyguard."

"Yes, dear, he is," Margaret countered.

"How am I going to run my shop with John Wayne here snapping at my heels?" Cassandra asked.

Reilly crossed his arms over his chest. John Wayne, huh? Well, he guessed there were worse things than being compared to his boyhood hero.

"Cassandra, Mr. Murdock is a professional. This is what he does for a living. And he isn't only your bodyguard. He's going to be investigating this situation—"

Her daughter's rigid posture would've made a drill sergeant proud. "There is no situation."

"Darling, I'm worried. Too many odd things have happened since you got back from your trip to Europe."

Reilly walked to the edge of the muted Oriental carpet that defined the sitting area. "What trip?"

Cassandra whirled around.

Damn, those eyes again.

The varying shades of green, changing from a light aqua to the darkest jade, reminded him of the ocean he'd seen while on an island in the Caribbean. Of course, he'd been looking through a scope of a high-powered assault rifle most of the time.

"Excuse me?" she said.

"When did you go to Europe? Did you travel alone and why?"

"August, yes." Cassandra snapped out her one-word answers. "And none of your damn business!"

"Cassandra Margaret!"

Reilly hid a grin as the beautiful creature in front of him attempted to rein in her temper by pressing her lips into a thin line. Her efforts did little to diminish the heat in her eyes or the bright pink tint on her cheeks.

Okay, she was hot. He could admit that. And after reading the information Digger had provided, he did see it pointing in the direction of something strange going on in the lady's life, but that still didn't mean he wanted to be here.

"I need a drink." Cassandra took a step around him and headed for the floor-to-ceiling bookcases on the far wall. "Mother?"

"No, thank you, dear. Would you like something, Mr. Murdock?"

Glancing over his shoulder, Reilly saw Cassandra's hand still over the crystal decanters. "Whatever Miss Van Winter is having is fine with me. And please, call me Reilly."

"Are you sure you won't sit down?" Margaret asked with a smile. "I think we may be in for a long siege."

Reilly returned her smile and walked to the sofa. He gripped his knee and sat, praying it wouldn't give out. Grateful to find the throbbing pain absent for the moment, he looked up to a glass half filled with ice and a smoky brown liquid. "Thank you."

Whiskey, he guessed. He was surprised by Cassandra's choice of liquor, but perhaps this afternoon's narrow escape was bothering her more than she was willing to admit. And with good reason.

"Will you tell me about your trip now?" he asked.

"Mr. Murdock, I don't believe we've established your need to know yet." Cassandra moved to the other side of the coffee table.

Reilly reined in his temper, reminding himself that the society princess had only found out a little over an hour ago she had a bodyguard. "Look, I can find out what happened with or without your help. This'll go a lot better if you work with me."

Dropping into the chair next to her mother, Cassandra took a sip of her drink. She ignored him and turned to her mother. "Mom, this is crazy."

"No, it's not." Margaret covered her daughter's hand with

her own. "What's going on is crazy, and you have to admit it. Please, let him help you."

"You don't know this man from Adam." Cassandra waved her glass in his direction. "Where did he come from? How did you find him? Can you trust him?"

Okay, that hurt.

Reilly's fingers tightened on his glass. Damn, he'd give anything to be back in bed with more than just this splash of booze. What he wanted was another bottle of Tequila. Correction, a bottle of 100 proof Mexican Blue Agave Tequila Reposado. None of that cheapo stuff for him again. If he was going to get good and drunk, he might as well splurge for the best of the best.

The bed didn't matter.

His bed.

Her bed.

Whoa, scratch that.

Reilly eyed the glass in his hand. It wasn't a bottle, but it would do. He swirled the contents once before lifting it to his lips, emptying it in one mouthful. He braced for the slow burn of expensive booze, so the taste of sweetened tea on his tongue was a shock.

Lowering the glass, he caught Cassandra's arched brow of triumph, and he offered a small salute in return. *Score one for the lady.*